REFE[

Gerry Bradley is an amazing author who writes from his heart and soul. His strong love for life and people comes through in each of his stories and his "Chit-Chat-Café" series definitely shows this. He will captivate, take you through the many lives of people Gerry has met along the way and I guarantee, you will not want to put this book down.

> Doreen Nygren
> Of – SSA Pacific
> A Carrix Enterprise
> Tacoma, Washington

I first met Mr. Bradley in 1995. As time passed we became friends and he told me about his writing and gave me copies of some of his articles. Needless to say, I look forward to the "Chit-Chat-Cafe". I am sure all his readers will enjoy!

> Kay Sharp
> Law Offices of – Christopher A. Benson
> Federal Way, Washington

The pleasure of reading your stories comes from the joy you so obviously get from hearing and of others life experiences. I have been struck by your sincerity as you, listen to others tell their stories.

> Jamie Cable
> Tacoma, Washington

Gerry's courage and perseverance through life is so apparent in his first book, "Birds From, the Thicket". His astute memory for the slightness of details and his keen sensitivity, make Gerry an unbelievable story teller. From his early childhood days in Oklahoma, his travels through young adulthood, and into the present, he is able to bring the reader along for his incredible journey. Gerry will make you laugh, cry and perhaps remember important treasures about your own journey through life.

I know that he brought all home to me.

Judy Heier
Downtown Business/Property Owner
Puyallup, Washington

Gerry Bradley is a hero who has been fighting the battle of chemical imbalance with some high degree of determination and obviously some equally high degree of success. His writing shows his determination to take life by the horns, and his personal successes are comparable to some professionals who have the same affliction and who have chosen to write of their own lives. His observations of the human condition indicate an intense interest in humanity and a sharp evaluation of what makes us tick.

Jay Taylor
Retired Industrial Arts Teacher
Queen Anne High
Seattle, Washington

Gerry has steadfast determination and unrelenting energy in behalf of his purpose ...a writer with heart and mind and soul that relates to this bound volume of world-wide short stories for all to read and enjoy throughout.

John Doty
Retired Teacher and Avid Reader

Gerry embraces life with vitality and eagerness found in few. Teacher, Radio Personality, salesman, raconteur – not only lives life but realizes a life fully lived.

Ruth Jenkins,
Recruiting Manager
Of: Robert Half Finance & Accounting
Seattle, Washington

Gerry is a truly gifted writer. And thanks for his sharing his writing for all…looking forward to his next, "Chit-Chat-Café" and its world-wide short stories.

> April Arnold
> Avid Reader of Puyallup, Washington

He is a writer, a prose writer, one that writes cogently above all can and does tell stories through his writing unlike any other. In fact there are few that write prose, but Gerry does and it is worth reading I assure you.

> Mike Dillon
> Publisher and Owner of Pacific Publishing
> Seattle, Washington

It is your heart that impressed me. After all of these years, your heart is still the thing I remember most about you. Heart is the thing that you have and that comes through the most in your writing.

> Jon Winter
> Consultant in Wildlife Biology
> Santa Rosa, California

Once a "Bird From, the Thicket" now set free to fly…away of thanking you for getting me started on the way to becoming an author! Now my dream has come true too. A special, that came out of your book. Gerry's songs have been resurrected by your writing the book! You're free indeed to go forth and help others, who have also been caught by the snare of the thickets.

> Karlese Prince
> Soon to be the author of –
> "In My Designer Shoes"

Gerry Bradley's stories bring back memories from the depths of your memory. All of us can find something familiar in the stories of life that Gerry communicates.

Kenton Spading
Co-Author,
Of: Amelia Ear hart's Stories
St. Paul, Minnesota

Garry Bradley

Now an author
of two books

CHIT - C H A T- CAFE

BOOK - I

Yarns from the Heart

Gerry Bradley

authorHOUSE®

AuthorHouse™
1663 Liberty Drive
Bloomington, IN 47403
www.authorhouse.com
Phone: 1-800-839-8640

First published by AuthorHouse 8/31/2009

ISBN: 978-1-4490-1100-0 (sc)

Printed in the United States of America
Bloomington, Indiana

This book is printed on acid-free paper.

FOREWORD

For those of us who have discovered optimism to be a tight vessel on life's seas, Bradley's book provides a refreshing narrative navigation. We all have stories, all of us have traveled the course behind those who have gone before; and it's helpful, comforting perhaps, when standing at the fork to be aware of what has laid ahead for others when they chose. Some chose well, but one must choose. After all, at some time things will get worse and it's possible for things to get better. Bradley did not give up. As the Russians say when pulling on the oars for safe harbor in the storm, "pray; but do not, stop rowing."

Robert G. Bauer
Attorney At Law

DEDICATION

I want to share how grateful I am to my wife, Sandra who has proven to be the best C.E.O. and a great influence as an editor, not to mention all of the arduous work she accomplished in setting the entire story to send on to the publisher.

And a big thanks to Dr. Ann Barber for her ability to further check and edit the book throughout. Both have proven to be total professionals and the anchor needed to ready the contents for final publishing.

And to round out our team effort, my son, Chris Scharmer agreed to be the illustrator sharing his innate talents for the entire series.

Once again I am privileged to have each and every one of you share your stories - allowing me to paint with words your accounts, which will bring future readers to realize more of the human spirit.

None of this could have come had it not have been for your constant support and belief regarding all that I continued to accomplish - which each of you can rightfully claim, has become a large part of the whole effort.

Bob Brauer said he was more than pleased to prepare the Foreword. All his comments couldn't have been finer. May he know how much I appreciate, the times he has taken to convey his complete, support and guidance, and encouragement.

And don't let me forget Lynn Benson; I have the weekly opportunity to work with as I step into the booth, to present my weekly program on KLAY RADIO here in our community. He has always proved to be the best anchor for me, so "Chit-Chat" can be shared with all of you my listeners each week.

May all of you enjoy each of the stories.

PREFACE

It doesn't matter what your job or profession happens to be. Yours may be: of those in industry, business and the professional world; and important blue collar workers, certainly classmates of yesterday, even those of unfolding Seniors yarns; and those in the sports world and certainly our militaries sagas from - the wars and important missions having to be completed.

They are your stories that you may have wanted to share with others for a long time. I am gladly accepting the honor of sharing every yarn.

My hope is that you'll see yourselves and more, in every one of them, as you read and share them. These are who I am about to reveal to you. They are the yarns conveyed to me, as I interviewed each of them. I am calling them *Yarns from, the Heart.*

AUTHORS NOTES

When thinking of all that has happened, I know this ride began years ago, and I wrote about it extensively, in my account of the first ride down the California Coastline, from San Rafael, California bound southward to Vandenberg A.F.B. California. It was only three-hundred and forty seven miles in length, another ride or quest that became mine. For years, I have watched others make it from the coast of California, and continue across the country, the good old U.S.A. They have done it in record time. I had a different idea or plan than theirs though.

Mine has developed over the years - of making the same ride. Instead, I have wanted not only to make the ride on a bicycle as before, I have known all along that the reason was far more than to make it, I have wanted and not even known it at first , to meet the people throughout the journey. That is precisely what occurred years before. I became acquainted with the people all the way down the coastline. However; that trip and time in my life took me another route - the route was highway 101.

Now the overall destination planned, is to do more than the miles, and the sighting of the land of the country, no, I wanted to meet the people where they were. And by doing this, I would be able to keep a running log and gain all of their stories mile by mile. Later, I would be able to share the findings with all that read the accounts.

Time and the bodily needs change through the years as one and all know. Other facts come such as the finding of asthma, allergic breakdowns, high blood pressure, arthritis in the knees and hips and back, not to mention the importance of insuring that I take all of the medications needed, to contend with all ahead through the miles and experiences throughout the sojourn of sojourns. Then, the encountering those that are bound to assault their own faults and actions, that would either endanger me or the team regarding the miles we take daily. All too many, as the recent couple that faced the dangers, and one was run over by another - to find his traveling companion left not only without her companion, husband, making their trip of all trips, but to have foiled the dream they had for years.

What has happened instead, is meeting the people, as I referred to, I have been able to meet them right here, in the greater area of The Pacific Northwest. I have met them as I have prepared copy for: the newspapers - magazines - books - and even the opportunity of my own radio program, for a period of some four years with a local radio station. Additional outlets have come in the recent days via Classmates not found before. And at the same time, I continue to meet vast numbers about, that seem to have their own saga to share. I have come to realize, I can meet the original goal or peddling the distance, that it would have taken through the cranks, hills, mountain ranges, plateaus, not to mention the weather changes, as I made way daily to reach the destination of the East Coast - now, I could do the same by interviewing one and all, writing of their accounts, yarns of their quests. In truth, doing this would prove as fascinating and would enable me even more miles than ever anticipated before. Now, I could literally travel worldly.

I wouldn't be confined only to the U.S.A. and its people. I would be able to draw from them - "The People and their Stories" throughout the world. For more of their adventures that would be coming daily. One of the true sources is coming from hooking up to classmates from the high schools I attended and graduated from, the college experiences and degrees I earned. Then there were those I met, and was stationed with during my enlistment while serving in the United States Air Force, even to the varying places and companies I had worked for throughout the years. I can see, and traverse a far more distant journey and be able to tell it through all of the tales gained, and not have to deal with the varying health conditions that more than likely would have stopped me from meeting the goal as dreamed of in the beginning.

Imagine, being able to travel as such through others trips, and lives, even to join them in their quests. Much more has happened. Now, I am able to vicariously join all of them, as they have taken much deeper trips or rides in their own lives. Examples that I can tell you about will stagger your minds.

To even think, that I could share in depth history of POW's from all of the wars they have fought in, been captured and lived through alone, would have to leave you in awe. And then to be able to have the company of the VETS Veterans that represented the fighting, men and women, through each of their campaigns reported is equally mind blowing, if that isn't enough, imagine being able to travel among six men that have a goal and are setting it by taking their journey through the miles at sea, through The Northwest Passage, all the way from Halifax, Nova Scotia, and upon facing all the travail daily and nightly aboard a fifty-eight foot sailing craft that hopefully, will see them clear to reach the Embarcadero, in the San Francisco Bay by this coming October. And to further be able to do this by keeping a log of my own of their ride, through much more than the seas, the ice bergs, the weather, the hard disciplined work that will tax all of the strength and beyond without question, to hope as they do, to have constant storms throughout, for that will break the way for them through the ice - the wildlife, such as the polar bears to name only one, and to have the smoother seas and warmer conditions, as they find they have made it through the passageway, and are headed southward to warmer seas and conditions.

And when thinking of not only that quest, but through the skilled, knowledgeable hearts and hands and fingers of two, who have found their own passion of playing for others, of a favorite of "Ragtime Piano Duo" throughout the country.

The more the gales continue, and the elements are faced, I am finding the travels, passions, of all of whom I am meeting a long the way. Not only are they sharing their lives, they are sharing what has been in their hearts and souls much the same.

Today, I can listen closely to each and hear the same exhilaration come from them, as they tell me their chronicles, to hear of their enthusiasm, their joy of finding their passions, and being able to practice them, but far more important, to share them with those, in their paths.

So you see, through only a few examples found, I am able to ride the ride of a life time with many more than hoped for, or expected, as I had originally planned. Thanks to them for their sharing as they have. I can more importantly share with all of you my readers today and in the future.

May all of you enjoy more than their epics, the wind in their faces, it blowing the wisps of their hair, the bronzed tanning of their bodies, the wear of and pain within, all that comes from what they give me the privilege to share with you, and share with you I shall, through "Chit-Chit-Café", and the ensemble of named titles and stories alike. I hope for all of you the same joy and wondering what will come next as you turn the pages. Happy reading to all of you!

PRO-VERB

My life is but a weaving between my Lord and me, I can not choose the colors He, work-eth steadily…The dark threads are as needful In the Weaver's Skillful hand as the threads of gold and silver in the pattern He has planned.

Anonymous

Table of Contents

YARNS FROM THE HEART

My life is a joy, filled with love, fun and friendship,
all I Need to do is stop all criticism, forgive, relax
and be Open.

Morning - Noon - or for that matter Night, was the perfect meeting place for each and every one of them. They had been meeting there for years. The truth was their friendships did anything but miss a beat.

Admittedly, I came a long later, but even I became a fixture in their eyes. My stops came to be as regular as theirs - ambling in for chit and chat for them.

The place became their spot of all spots. It reminded me of a place I had been before while traveling east after my first year of college. I was taking a month to see the country, I hadn't experienced before while traveling east.

This journey was after attending my first year of college work. I was taking a month or more to get out and see the country I hadn't experienced before.

There are memories for many of us that might go the same way as well. I had been moving eastward toward my destination on the east coast. This was anything but the halfway point, out there in South Dakota.

I was a typical California young man at this time in my life. As I pulled into this town, that had been there for many a year; I spotted the old timers in splintered captain chairs, leaning up against the wall.

I stepped up to enter the store and said, "howdy." They didn't even grunt. Both of them had earned every crease on their faces.

It didn't take long to find my pop and some munchies, pay the owner, and heard. "yuh come back, yuh hear." Those gents didn't say one thing.

I didn't forget them, seeing how one had his boots tangled in his chair. And the aroma of their corn cob pipes, sifted through the warm, summer air. I loaded and turned eastward down the road. As I cruised I thought of those old boys many times through the years.

When reflecting on that sighting, I was sure I knew what the place, time, for that matter, players were. That was the towns gathering spot. I was also sure they came and went every day, had time to sit in those chairs and chew the fat. That place became crowded with all of them, the men and women a like. They had gone to school together since they were kids.

So what could have been a better place for them to share their stories? It was where they could share, good and bad yes even their fish tales, with their arms stretched out, to make every one know their fish was that long. Thank God for these places, in all of our lives.

Just sitting there having my morning coffee and having said, "I'm having German breakfast (fresh blackberry pie) and you go ahead and heat it for me, I'll have the whip-cream."

Their hair had long before slid away. Outside, a couple of them with motorcycles, with all of the extras, others in their cars, even those in updated SUV'S, and pick-ups.

What I enjoyed was seeing them say with brimming smiles, laughter and hail, loudly to arrivers. "We've got our regular table this morning." They were like boys and girls sitting around the camp fire.

I turned back to my German breakfast and the frothing latte, to check out the sports section, in the newspaper.

I thought of those folks and how they enjoyed each others company.

Characters such as these will become the central point of "Yarns of the Heart."

FIRST DAYS OF HIS LIFE

(A SHORT STORY – A LETTER)

It's not something that occurs, everyday in our lives. You joined our family on July 11th 2008, thanks to your daddy Eric and your mother, Kristy. Your grandma was there also. Grandma's first child was your uncle Christopher and then your daddy twenty one months later. Grandma was so pleased to have both.

Something else Dylan, as your grandparents we soon found at birth you to be a big boy. When your Daddy was born he was ten pounds 11 oz., and twenty-one inches long. Your Grandmother thought she was going to be your Nana but claimed her true title, Grandma.

You are a binding force that has bound our family as one. We are so rich with you.

Your parents don't have any idea that Papa is writing this about you. One thing was apparent, your hands and feet were very large.

I immediately had you pegged for the future University of Washington to play on the basketball team. But your Daddy said, "No, volleyball." I didn't argue. It would be wonderful, to see you in the future Olympics. In truth, D. is what your mother called you from the beginning. The name or way she expresses best who you are is by saying, "I wouldn't have ever believed we would have such a beautiful boy." When hearing her I am warmed to the heart.

Dylan Cash, you are fortunate to have the most loving parents on the earth. We are grateful to have them as our son and daughter – not daughter-in-law, for, we have always felt your Mother is our daughter. We love her so much and we know you will your entire life.

Before continuing with your story, I want you to know more about your grandma. She grew up in Rochester, Minnesota. Grandma was an orphan and shortly afterwards, was adopted by your great-grandmother and your great-grandfather. They were Mr. and Mrs. Paul Baumgardt. Wait until you hear their story. When you do you'll be very proud of them.

Grandma had wonderful days, and more, with your great grandfather. We called him Grandpa Paul. He left us three years ago on June 10th 2006. He as you has been in our hearts as you will be forever.

You see, your great grandparents were married and selected property on the outskirts of Rochester, Minnesota. It was their dream to have a root beer stand out front of your great-grandfather's garden he designed, planted and cared for raising your grandmother little "miss sunshine", as she came to be known as. Grandma is going to tell you stories of her growing up that will delight you. She had her own special tree she played in as a little girl. Imagine seeing her climbing, and dangling on the branch. One day she was outside with her dad helping with the plants. She thought they were weeds, to find her dad say, "they're not weeds, they are plants, the same as people, and it's important to help them grow just as people." Grandma will tell you about the creek she and her neighborhood friends played in for hours beside the garden. We're so proud of your great grandfather who worked seven days a week for some sixty-seven years before he turned one-hundred and one years old. We miss him very much. I want you to remember some of his story. That way, when you become a parent you can pass these stories on to your children.

I want you to know you are to have some special times too. Your grandma is ahead of me already. She has been taking care of you as you have been growing bigger every day. It has been our gift, to your daddy and mother, to help out, making sure you were not with another, outside of our family, even though your parents had to work , all of us including another grandma (a treasured loving friend of your parents) has taken care of you during the week. Her name is Bonnie.

Grandma and I care for you every Sunday. It is a very special day for us.

Your parents and Grandma are about to take you on a far-a-way trip to Mexico! Papa is staying home working to get the new year of 2009 well on its way. To do all possible to ready the content of the book so it can be sent to his publisher.

I know you're going to have a wonderful time on your first vacation. Where you'll really have fun is around the swimming - pool. Grandma is looking forward to taking you in the pool every day. I'll miss all of you very much though. I'm lucky though, your photo is on my desk so I am reminded to tell you how much I love you every day.

You just celebrated your first holiday with us. It was thanksgiving. We had a fine, time. You sat there on Grandma's and Daddy's lap and we didn't hear a whimper from you.

I've wanted and planned to write this story all about you. I'm going to begin the book with your story because you are so important to all of us – that's right, one very important member of our family.

Your Daddy is really enjoying you to the core of his being. He is so proud of you. And so is your Mother. You get to go to see the doctor to get your shots – which cause you to cry. All that they do for you is so important. Why, you have gotten to take rides with them. You've been to their friends homes, shopping. You're going to be quite the traveler in no time.

Taking trips was how everything was for me to, when I was a little guy like you.

I've told you something about your Grandmother, now it's time for me to tell you something about me. I didn't come from Minnesota. I was born in the town of Enid, Oklahoma. I lived there with my mother, father and brother before coming to Seattle, Washington during the fifth grade.

When I was a little guy like you, I took special rides with my Daddy too. You see he drove a big truck full of what I came to know as soda pop. He delivered cases full of bottles of pop to many stores and towns around where we lived.

My Mother stayed home at first with both of us boys. We did all kinds of fun things together. We played with all of the kids in the neighborhood. Later, my mother taught me how to cook and bake – yes sir, I used to bake cakes. What was really fun was learning to fish. Mother was the one that taught me how to fish and we went fishing and caught lots of fish.

One more thing, my mother taught me what the name of every flower around our house in Enid was. I came to know every one of them. They had strange names: pansies, nasturtiums, gladiolas, zinnias, daisies, and roses. I loved squatting down with Mother so she could tell me all about the plants. That was really fun!

Right now you like to eat, drink from your bottle full of warm milk, sleep, rock, play with your toys in your seat, even mess your pants. It's ok though, that's what you should do. After all, you're doing all of that so you can grow up to be a big, healthy boy.

Remember me telling you about your daddy and mother who had to work. Your daddy works in a big building with other people, it's a big place full of everything (one way to think of it is – "soup to nuts"). It's called home depot. And your mother works around a lot of cars every day. She takes care of what you will learn about called money. And she and your daddy are very good workers.

As we watch you grow every day, I have been thinking about all kinds of fun things I'm waiting to share with you.

Ever since hearing of your coming, I have had some pretty important things to tell you. To some they might be thought of as too hard for you to understand. I don't! I am going to share them with you many times. Right now it's too early. I'll have to wait for you to grow to be a big boy. You'll be taller and weigh quite a lot more, but I believe able to understand what Papa is telling you then.

These are some of things I want for you most. Before I tell you, I want you to know all of your family. I knew from the start you were quite the young man. You are already making your Daddy and Mother and Grandmother very proud of you. You are very tall to all of us already!

I know all of us want you to discover so much for yourself as you grow older. At the same time every one of us, hope, to teach and share many things with you. We want to help you in every way we possibly can. We hope what we teach you will be things that you will be able to carry with you every day of your life.

Dylan Cash I'm thinking as your Daddy is, "when you get somewhat older" we'll be able to share so much more with you.

I want to teach you to know about how important things are like: little birds, squirrels, other little animals, just to name a few. One of the wonderful things that you'll find out about your daddy, is he always used to help the little people. He was just like you, one great big boy compared to the other kids. One of the stories you'll hear about him was when he was playing soccer. His mother was a spectator. She couldn't understand why your Daddy just stood out on the soccer field and didn't move. She asked, "Why don't you move?" To hear him reply, "I didn't want to hurt the kids smaller than me."

I have been very fortunate to be Dad for your Daddy and Christopher for a long time. I want you to know I have and always will love both of them very much.

Some things I know that will help you in the biggest ways are, the kind of things you can carry with you forever. They're lessons I learned from my Mother were she here, she would assure you she loves you. Larry, my stepfather would feel the same about you. Both of them left us nearly twelve years ago.

My mother taught me lessons that helped me more than I would have ever have imagined. She taught me big words and ways to behave. I learned words as: please, thank you, your welcome, nice words – yes mam' and yes sir, excuse me – you'll really need that when you burp. Others, such as I'm sorry, make sure you mean it when you say it though. I knew how important it was, to look people in their eyes. These seem simple. They are in a way. But you'll be able to carry them and share them every where you go from now on.

D. I want you to always say how much you appreciate just being alive. Every day! And I also want you to learn how important it is for you to be sure to laugh and enjoy every day too, and to make your own choice, to pray, thank god for all you have. I'm going to bring your attention to all kinds of books. These are going to be important for you.

Other things I hope to bring you to know are: what I call how important a fish bowl is, because you are always going to be seen when you least, expect it. Time and again you'll be facing that word choice, and what it means in your life. I know by teaching you these things your life will be easier for you, no matter how old you are.

I hope I can teach you how to save and why it is so important. I know these are big things, but I know how smart you are.

Remember what I told you about, they're called, "old fashioned manners." Papa tried to practice them all the days of his life. I don't know what would have come of me had I not been taught these I am sharing with you. I have applied them everywhere I've been Dylan Cash.

Papa and Grandma grew up in a different time than your Daddy and Mother. It's lucky, because the thing that both of your parents appreciate about us, is they have known we have tried in every way possible to remain young, able, even interested in all they do. We are you know. We have seen and experienced a lot as your Daddy and Mother have. For instance your Daddy loves to deal with all kinds of electronic things. And your Mother is a very smart person. She is good when it comes to taking care of you, making sure your Daddy knows how much she loves him, us to. Your Mother is a whiz, when it comes to a subject you're going to learn a lot about, mathematics or some call it math and much more.

Both your parents are wonderful employees. D. They have "got it all together" not to leave out your Grandma for she is a very smart, intelligent woman. Every one of us, have our strong points. Where I am the strongest is, I am what you and others call a creative guy. I love to write! It's like painting with words for me. And you'll find what I write is in books for people to read and enjoy, and learn from as well.

You'll come to know that all people you meet are his or her own person. That's so important for you to learn. Probably the last thing I want to help you with, is to know that even though everyone is different, it is still important to accept each person, to get a long with all, to reach out to as many as you can. To help, and to be, willing, to give to others.

Finally, I was thinking because the world changes so fast, I told your grandma the other night, "you know something, Dylan Cash may even go to mars," another planet, which you will learn about. He might even go there to live." No matter where you go, the most important thing, I want to share with you, is how deeply you are loved today and all the days ahead.

One, more, thing, remember it isn't right to hit girls!

Whoops – I must make sure that you have these additional gifts. Now I've got you wondering don't I, like a surprise, or one of those times that I have shared with you, the same as "jack in the box" jumping out to surprise you with: family outings, trips to the zoo, the circus, a trip to a farm, a book store so you can see all the adventures in them and also the library, to sit with other children for the story time hour, sledding as your Daddy and uncle got to do when they were little boys, to climb trees, to learn all about your Grandma's garden and flowers which she loves and will want to share with you, time to look at all of the families photos, especially, photo books your Grandma has kept of you since you joined us.

We want you to learn how to ride a bike using trainer wheels, to watch programs grandma and I have collected for you to enjoy with all of us, to learn so many other things that daddy is going to teach you. He'll help you learn how to shoot baskets, to hit the volleyball over the net, to fly a kite, to have adventures as I did when I was a little boy. I want you to learn to cook with your grandma and your mommy. Probably the most important is, to learn how to hit a ball, slide in at home base and have dirty britches of course, to hold your first baseball glove up to your face and smell the leather. You can do the same in a western store when smelling the leather in a saddle. Daddy will teach you how to tie knots, climb ropes to fish, to know what a joy it is going to be to catch your very first fish, to hike and climb hills. Now you're getting the idea of all you can and will be able to do. What fun we're all going to have! And through all of it, every one of us, are going to get lots of hugs and kisses from you, the greatest gifts of all. You know you can't get enough of them! It's all going to be a wonderful adventure, we can all share with one another, because we love you so very much Dylan Cash.

Love your Papa

A TEACHER'S BELIEF IN ME

*Saying something helps you believe In, it Doing
something helps others believe In you.*

I know there is one teacher and guide that came in your life too.
The one I want to share with you came in my earlier days; it has been
my fortune to more than remember him. He has become the finest
friend ever. It is with candor, I can say I have come to love him through
all of these years. John Doty is the finest man I ever met. There is
much to say about him. He was my English teacher, a beacon for
me. His work was more like ministry for students not only there at
Queen Anne High – truthfully, he continued doing the same while at
Seattle Community College in Seattle, Washington. I didn't have the
opportunity to remain, see or hear more reports of others that attended
either of the two schools. Nor did I have the privilege to graduate with
my class of 1959, for my parents announced during my junior year they
were moving to Northern California mid-year of my junior year. After
I left and made way to Northern California to rejoin my family in San
Rafael, California changes came for John Doty and me. He continued
working with the students at Queen Anne High and later accepted the
opportunity to teach at Seattle Community College, where he became
the head of the Humanities Department. I continued my work in my
senior year and graduated with the class of 1959 at San Rafael High.
Mr. Doty didn't just teach, he guided his students as he had me, and
was a prominent figure for college students to earn their Associate Arts
Degrees.

I found later, when he wasn't working with students and staff through the years, time passed and finally he retired. What angered me was hearing that after all of that dedication, he was never "given a gold watch" or for that matter, received any comments or acts of thanks for all of his service. When hearing that, I knew if I didn't do anything from that moment forward, I would see that this and much more would occur.

John Doty, I believe, without even a slight pause, I am going to see that your story, is, to be an entry one in the series of World-Wide short stories, of, "Chit-Chat-Café". Sir, you have earned'it. I pray you will see and read this as the rightful commemoration for all you did, in my life, and in so many others, that you taught through the years.

We're always hearing the same truth or plea that teachers don't earn near what they should. Consequently, John had to work as his colleagues to care for his family during the off months. He was ambitious, working with a fellow teacher accepting bids to paint the expansive homes on Queen Anne Hill. Even though I wasn't there, I had the same experiences of painting as they. But, when hearing how he took the steps up and down on lengthy ladders, scaling the sides of the homes and painting them, I knew that was how he earned for his family on the down months, before returning to the classroom each school year.

As he told me this, I could imagine how tenuous it had to be for him, no scaffolding, just thin rings. I could see him swaying there in the wind, brush in one hand, a, bucket of paint in the other to get the job done. I know he would have been a sight to see in his coveralls splashed with the colors of paint from day to day, sweat pouring from his brow. That is only one facet of this mans life, for he is one that never ducked one task when it was in his path.

You'll read now of how this friendship took place on a day never forgotten, as I introduced him in my first book, *Birds From - The Thicket*. It was my sophomore year.

I changed his name for the sake of protection to Jim Daily, in truth his true name is Mr. John Doty.

Jim Daily, has been and remains a significant teacher and was a crowning Bird that helped turn the tide, affecting my thought of pursuing furthering education. You had to come to know him, as we did, during our sophomore year in high school. I can still see him standing in front of the class with his suspenders that he wore every day. One day, he, shared with us why he chose to wear suspenders, instead of a belt. His story called attention to his father, who made him know wearing suspenders was a must to retaining tight abdomen muscles. There wasn't one snicker.

Our classes were rolling along, when he assigned us to select a favorite book of our choice. We were to read and write a book review. Reading, wasn't my favorite, but was about to become more than a favorite, as I found Ernest Hemingway's *The Old Man and The-Sea*. From the moment I picked up the book, I began reading and became enthralled in the story line, to the point of carrying and reading the book everywhere I went.

I knew that evening was our families' night to join my grandparents for dinner. As you guessed, I took the book and continued to read it, before and during our dinner. This was something for me, as we were dining at our favorite fish house, Crawford's, down on Elliott Way, also in Seattle. What could have been more fitting, to be reading about this, the largest fish "I've ever caught", and looking at the Captain's Plate I had ordered.

Jesse introduced me to a Champion Billiards player from Chicago, at the Marine Firemen's Union. He taught me the game called pool. I was clumsy when it came to handling the cue stick. When I first met him, I would no more have thought of featuring his life in a future assignment as this book review, than could be imagined.

Our family was conversing as usual, where I could have been joining in, I was bent over the print, captive, to Hemingway's style and story line about this old man, and his triumph, he had finally caught.

The day the assignment was due, I turned my paper in along with my fellow students. It was a couple of days later that Mr. Daily stood in front of the class and shared the results. We thought he was finished and he said, "There was one paper that stood out above all of the others; I can tell you the writer of this paper exhibits, he, will be an up and coming writer in the future." By now all of us were plain curious, even to hear one of the girls pipe up and say, "Who is it?" Mr. Daily said, "It's, Gerald's paper." Then another asked if it was, and he said, "No it's Gerald Kent's and I'm going to ask him to come up and share his paper with our class." I had never been asked to do anything like this before, but now I walked to the front of the class, and he handed my paper to me. All eyes and ears were on me, as I read the entire paper. Afterwards, their comments were nothing but, "What a wonderful piece of writing it was." To think, that this one English teacher, had recognized the effort made. That moment, continued to ring down the hallways, as my fellow students exited our class. Before we were dismissed, Mr. Daily asked me to explain to the class, why, I, took the direction I had taken; I shared my background about my friend from the Marine Firemen's Union, and how he taught me billiards, that he lived much the same as in *The Old Man and The - Sea* in an shanty, down on the Dwamish River. When they heard this, they could see, how I, came to write the paper. Here, was an absolute turnabout for me! From that point forward, I considered continuing pursuing my degree.

What I learned from this, was this would be carried much like a torch, to light my future student's efforts, as they progressed in their educations and beyond. In my case, I pursued my Associate Arts Degree, while attending Allan Hancock College in Santa Maria, California. Then, I continued to California Poly Technical College in San Luis Obispo, for the summer session. Upon graduating with my AA degree, I sent applications to colleges and universities throughout the west, and arrived at the decision to complete my under graduate work at, Seattle Pacific College in Seattle, Washington, where I gained my BA degree, at long last with the class of 1973.

And, to think, the direction or embers were lighted by this man, I, have introduced to you, that saw to my having found him, a teacher, that had belief in me.

ODYSSEY of ANOTHER AUTHOR FROM ENID

*Frequently, the difference between Success and
Failure, is the resolve To stick to your plan and long
Enough, to win.*
- David Cottrell

All began in the early forties in Enid, Oklahoma. Life was simpler then. The lifestyle was far better than ten to fifteen years before. Those older had experienced dreadful moments that couldn't but be deep in their fiber. It was a time that had not been washed away from their minds – hearts – or souls.

Younger generations as mine, seven to eight years old, heard relatives accounts experienced first hand. They told me about the devastating drought, that hit our part of the country, the southwest. It affected all for years, through the depression sifting through all of society. It, was a degenerating kind of condition, that marked the land. It scourged and burned the land completely. John Steinbeck wrote about it, and named it, *The Grapes of Wrath*.

None of this can be told ignoring any of those days. It touched far more than the earthen soil. It was ingrained in the very hearts and souls of all in those years. Those of that country of Oklahoma, Texas, Arkansas, Kansas, Nebraska, even sweeping on to Washington D.C. never forgot the devastation from that era. The time, revealed, the hollowness of the howling wind, the intensity of the black cloud that never seemed to disappear, as it swept across the country. Photographs revealed the harsh times, the lost look, the creases of their faces, ragged clothing, a look of sheer hunger in the children's eyes, a splintered, hopeless look.

The writer, I, remembered, wrote short stories in *The Saturday Evening Post*, and *Collier's Magazine,* that my mother used to share with me. I suppose you could say, his stories got to me. It must have permeated my soul. For, I am the writer, I, undoubtedly wanted to be. One more incite came. The radio! I wanted my shot at the radio business too. Both came true.

While writing my first book, I also had the opportunity to write for newspapers in Washington and Oregon, and began writing for magazines. Ahead, would be plans, to, write, *"Chit-Chat-Cafe"* which would be world-wide short stories.

All of it brings me to think as one editor said, "Your writing evokes the depth of the "Red Earth of Oklahoma." An odyssey indeed!

Although I kept hearing, "You really should share with others, especially, new writers as yourself, fledgling authors, what path you took, to market your very first book."

After thinking about this, I thought, it might prove helpful for them as well. All involved similar paths, taken by other authors I am sure, yet there would be writers that might gain insight, as to how they might want to proceed.

Let me alert you to know, the writing is hard, ponderous, and as described by another, "The loneliest work in the world." Truthfully, what comes afterwards is far more arduous. Even though you have practiced the definition of a writer, "To become a writer requires that you write every day." Ahead, comes how to market your work. Where and how to start, are your first questions that you wrestle with I assure you.

My market plan unfolded this way. I knew from the start, if there was any key, it had to be, never stop, no matter how many bulwarks might come. And come they came.

Although, when hearing other writers say, "You know you have to publish to be published," could have stopped me right there and then. It didn't. Quite honestly their words were motivators. I knew I had been published before while writing as a member of the yearbook staff at Allan Hancock Junior College in Santa Maria, California. The assignment I, was to write about the founder of the college, Allan Hancock. To do this, brought me to find not only did I love, writing, I equally thrived over the process of first interviewing, those who knew him best, his wife and his closest friend – his "Chief cook and bottle washer."

But, I thought further, I knew another way I might be published. I had grown up in, the Queen Anne Hill area in Seattle, Washington. I remembered my grandfather used to receive the newspaper, *The Queen Anne News*. So, I looked the phone number up, and called, asked to speak with the editor, and heard, "You're in luck, I'm the editor." And, to this day, (one, that has become not only my mentor, but a good friend).

I shared that I had written my book, a full draft; however, I had extracted six sequels from it, about my days as a boy living on lower Queen Anne Hill, known as (the Uptown) and above the hill, while attending Queen Anne High School from the eighth grade through my Junior year. He replied, "You send them to me, I'll read them, then let you know, if we're going to publish them." I heard a few days later, "I really like what you have written, and I am going to publish all six." You can imagine how pleased I was over this news. And that was only the beginning, while polishing the draft and adding more to it.

From that moment and the query, I was given the opportunity to not only do, this, I followed it up, by asking, if I could be considered as a guest columnist for the newspaper. And it was granted. Consequently, I wrote for the paper for two and a half years or the like. My column included my going back to the old neighborhood of yesterday, and viewing as it was then, compiling the facts and writing of my view throughout the community. It was well received.

And, not that long afterwards, I found another newspaper to the south. It was *The Federal Way News*. I approached the editor much the same way. As it turned out, now, I, was writing for two newspapers, this time, the same format and more, for I researched and wrote, as to how it had been compared to the current day. This was read and enjoyed by many. I knew this, for they told me this throughout the area.

Next a similar from *The Bonney Lake Times*. That brought my copy going out into three newspapers; I continued to ready my drafted version of *Birds From, The Thicket*, to be sent on to my publisher, Authorhouse, in Bloomington, Indiana.

If you can recall the measure was to be published elsewhere. I had done that. And one day I thought, I might as well try to syndicate and write for additional newspapers. I readily knew, I didn't have contact with what I called "The Big Boys", and found Self Publishing. After reading more, I decided I would try to do this. The next step was, to send queries throughout the west, and doing this required far more than the written word. I was calling small and medium sized newspapers every day.

From that effort, I finally received a positive response, shortly afterwards, I was working within the community of Astoria, Oregon, where I had a wonderful opportunity to write for *The Daily Astorian, a* much larger newspaper. And due to this I was writing for newspapers in Washington and Oregon.

To do this, required my wife and I to traverse back and forth, into what became my beat. It was perfect, for I covered the Oregon coast from Astoria to Cannon Beach, and communities up and down that portion of the coastline. We made way there every month, or no later than two months. It couldn't have been more perfect, I gathered the look of the peoples, the area, all, that was going on throughout, and my wife went shopping. Afterwards, I had enough to write copy for the Saturday – monthly edition, which I had my column in for nearly a year.

What came afterwards, was, contacting one local radio station, and the surprise was, to receive my own radio program, which I had for approximately four years. And to think, that the original request was, to merely share some of what I had written. The writing took another form though. I called my program, "Chit-Chat" of which my format was covering writings, a broad survey of events occurring, throughout the local scene and highlights of news throughout the country and beyond. So, finally I, gained what I, had aspired for years prior, as a boy. Although, before, completing my degree-work in college, I, had, an equal opportunity, to be the News Broadcaster, through campus for the fellow students. And you might say, what, else was a part of the marketing plan that unfolded.

I approached my home town newspaper, The Enid News Eagle in Enid, Oklahoma, and introduced my book and inquired, as to their willingness to publish a piece in the newspaper, to make the readers aware, of a long before Home Town boy's efforts.

They confirmed and made arrangements for me to have a telephone interview with one, Robert Baron, who wrote a fine piece that hit the front page of the newspaper, November 5th, 2005; the result was, a line in front of the Hastings Book Store for interested readers to obtain their copy of the books. At the same time, five radio stations covered the book throughout North Western Oklahoma. And, that, led me to corporate, for Hastings books in Amarillo, Texas.

The intent was, to provide, coverage in five additional book stores throughout Northwestern Oklahoma. And from there, I found the potential was to reach into sixteen states across the country, and 144 book stores with Hastings Book Stores. The hold up was a depleted budget. But at the same time, we found a comparable insurance package as such, which, would have enabled the following: with this, we would have had the opportunity to carry the book next, into the North West Region, to include the home state of Washington, Oregon, and Idaho even into Montana.

What I am pronouncing is if future writers and authors want and are willing, the vast opportunities are there by staying the course.

Then, I proceeded by contacting both the schools and mental health sectors; whereby, I had opportunity to introduce, be considered the key note speaker, and accompanied by mental health officials to present both the book and all that was available for interested citizenry throughout North Western Oklahoma. That format was something that was possible not only there, but could have been available by

27

pursuing it the same way throughout the country. However; had I not continued "staying the course" none of this mentioned would have been possible. This still may be an opening in the future.

Yes, all that I have shared had and was occurring at the same time.

The latest is to introduce both the first book discussed on a website, determine interested readers that want to obtain the book, take orders and send them to one and all. Paving the road, if you will, to my equivalent, of the previous books, *Chicken Soup Books.* All of this is pending and in the meantime one other thrust came. I was able to gain the opportunity to see my books placed at one neighboring Barnes and Noble and Borders Book Store. It was something when taking my wife to see it on the shelf. I'll never forget hearing her say, "Why, it's like receiving the Oscar."

While, all was, happening, I made total contact via Classmates and was able to get the word out, and they began to obtain copies of my book. Before I knew it, they exchanged it, and would you believe due to this, I know for a fact, my book went all the way across the pond into Scandinavia, specifically Denmark. So, it could be said, that my book was widespread without question.

A phenomenal finding has come; that is, I am gaining wonderful stories, that I fully intend to enter into the world-wide short stories that will soon be introduced.

My, hope is, each of you will pursue and keep the course as this one author did and does daily, fulfilling more miles of the Odyssey of one hailing from Enid.

A MAN IN HIS GARDEN

Success is not the key to happiness.
Happiness is the key, to success, if You love what you
are doing, you will be successful.
Albert Schweitzer

Sandra and I went back to be with her dad in Rochester, Minnesota, for his one-hundredth birthday. We rolled across the railroad tracks. I said, "Hold it" - and pulled over and I blurted out, "You know what, those tracks may be ones, I traveled when I was ten, to the Northwest. It wouldn't surprise me, that, I, saw, you, out there with your dad."

This was his special day.

It was only a short time ago that we heard he began to fall down. That became the decision maker, as one neighbor saw him lying on the knoll. Consequently, we moved him where he could receive care he deserved.

Today, the cakes were in place, the hall was regally decorated, and the ladies were busy, preparing food, coffee, and punch.

One said, "Here he comes!"

He hobbled in on his walker to hear a rousing applause from all. Tears rolled down his cheek; he had a pleasing warm look.

I couldn't look at him without remembering how I saw him walk Princess, his daschund, with a brimming smile, when he saw his Sandra and me, on my first visit. He wiped his brow and held his crumpled ball cap, leaned, caught his breath, and reached out to hug Sandra to reveal how happy he was to see her. He was wearing stained pants and a plaid shirt. His face was weathered, from his work in his garden.

Sandra told me how he worked the garden seven days a week.

I noticed his crinkled, long hands and fingers that were gnarled revealing arthritis, as he reached out to shake my hand. We hardly spoke before he said, Sandi, I'm so glad you came home, and I see you brought Gerry with you adding,"he's a tall one."

But today, we enjoyed looking on, as he welcomed all of his friends. He had shaved, revealing red cheeks. In fact, he looked sharp, in his navy, frayed sweater. His white wispy hair and recent hair-cut, and his bright blue eyes flashed, as they had in his youth. He smiled with glee as he stood there, looking at three-hundred friends.

My view of him was more like peering back to his homeland of Hundskops, Germany, where he sailed, on the SS Columbus, to berth in America at Ellis Island. He was twenty years old then. 'It wasn't that hard to believe I came over with Columbus," he jokingly said.

Paul Baumgardt's story began on November 14th 1904.

He grew up well before his time among his friends, and relatives. When he was eight years old, the men in his family marched off to fight in the World War I. He replaced them by caring for the geese, goats, chopping wood, and working in the grocery-tavern of his home town.

Hundskops was a village of two to three hundred people. These experiences readied him for all that was ahead.

He decided to leave his home, for America – realizing, the men relatives from the war, continually took his earnings. He knew remaining he couldn't win; so he made his plans to get away.

Upon his arriving in New York City, he traveled by rail for two days into Canada. On to Chicago, and from there, he made his way to Kenosha, Wisconsin, and joined other relatives.

Throughout his life, he was definitely a praying young man of deep faith. First, he worked on a of course doing landscape, later, he got a job in the Nash Motors plant doing mechanical work on the parts and drill press. While in Kenosha, Wisconsin he found work with the Simmons Mattress Company, in line seaming and sewing.

There he became ill with tuberculosis; he came under care from public charge and was assigned to the state sanitarium for treatment for six years. To think while there, he gained his citizenship, worked as a paid gardener, and received honors for his work.

After recovering, he headed for Milwaukie, Wisconsin with thirty-five cents in his pocket, uniting with a German Methodist family. There, he made and sold leather pocket books and purses throughout the community. He told me, "They paid me $15.00 for those pocket books!"

Afterwards, he met his bride and married in Wisconsin and stayed two years. They secured property where they lived with plans of developing a root beer stand, at the same time building – developing a garden/nursery. If that wasn't enough, he worked at the Mayo Clinic for fifteen years. While recovering from tuberculosis found he had serious arthritis. His work ethics kept him designing his garden, enabling those in the area to gather their vegetables and flowers for many years, where there was a steady string of traffic through the years, on Highway 14 east of Rochester, Minnesota.

What brought us was our vacationing for a few days, with full intent to spend as much time with her dad as possible.

Sandra shared one story she experienced as a little girl with her dad. While she was outside working with her dad helping to transplant, she didn't realize it, but was soon to learn, that the weaker plants she was throwing away, were in her dad's viewpoint, "Plants like people that need nurturing to grow and be healthy."

Throughout the community he had been known as "The Gardener of all Gardeners!" He'd been there for sixty-seven years, making certain all had fine produce and flowers. During winter seasons he could be found reading his bible, becoming versed in its contents, stories, and how it related to his life. And when I asked him each year, what I heard in reply was, "I just got my new catalogs to order seeds for the spring."

That was the first day being with him there in the garden. Before me was a mature ripe crab apple tree. Apples to reach and pluck and take a bite. I tried one and found it as the Okanogan, Washington apples of my boyhood.

I caught a glimpse of the blowing Fir, Colorado Blue-Spruce, and the flitting gray birds, feeding from the berries of the branches. The lawn revealed a close cut look, and the first frost was just around the corner.

I remarked, "I've heard about the nursery for years and I would love to see it."

His life had been one where he provided not only flowers and vegetables of prime value for his neighbors, he had grafted special plants with vibrant colors and unusual varieties.

No one including us could look at this special place hewn from the soil and not feel the seasons of life. Before us were: zinnias, roses, sunflowers larger in diameter than the sun itself, seedlings of saplings, rhubarb, beets, raspberries still on the vine, that fall in each persons fingers. There were lines of pine-trees, string beans ready to pick; along with red peppers, hot peppers, potatoes, horse chestnuts, strewn and cracked from the season itself. Not to mention, walnut trees, asparagus (white asparagus) only found at his nursery; strawberries, dahlias, cherry tomatoes stringing out on the vine lying, on the ground; miniature sunflowers, plants such as the variegated Maple trees.

As I write, I vividly recall seeing the grass hoppers beneath all of the plants. Crickets were striking their legs together bringing harmony for the evening. At the same time, I saw a squirrel clinging to the tree with its tail waving in the breeze to flag my presence, the chirping-singing birds throughout the trees and the brush where Sandi and her friends played years ago down on the creek.

I noted how Paul had outlived the railroad trains across the highway. I realized his dedication and spirit for life that continued to keep his weathered, clad look, with his baseball cap, layered clothes, rubber boots, gloves and soft loving voice, beckoning all to come and draw from his garden.

I knew from all I had seen, was evidence where one and all came to experience a deep-seeded peace on the earth.

A message that is heard over and over is, you knew Paul was going to be out there on his knees tending the garden, so he could provide not just stories, but true service in the community. He knew that his work was his way of readying all to reach everyone's tables.

That was then, now to be here with him watching him seated at center stage, thanking everyone at every table.

There were his German friends and it was warming to hear them converse in their native language. Many came because they had been children of his friends through the years. They wanted him to know, they came in their parents' places.

He didn't look one-hundred years old! He had to be here, for this day was a tribute of its own.

Afterwards, he began to tire, yet reached out to play for us on his mouth organ. What broke the moment and brought tears to our eyes, was hearing him play "America," after hearing all of his German tunes, and Christmas carols. We hugged and kissed him and wished him one more "Happy Birthday".

And today, we have come as all did for his birthday. This time, Paul is paid far more than respect, for all mentioned back then. Today, the family and friends, from years past, are here for celebrating his full life.

It looked as though he was going to make it to one-hundred and two years of vintage.

His stay with all of us changed, as he died on June tenth of 2006, when he had his last heart attack and nap. All of us were pleased, that he left us, just as he had hoped.

Here we all are joining hands on the green hearing some shed their tears, as to his no longer being here for all of us, and listening to special refrains of his favorite German hymns.

We now know that he is caring for the largest gardener of all, working far more and sharing each and everyone of his stories.

AN ELDERLY WOMAN'S STORY TO SAFETY

The world is a dangerous place.

An elderly woman had just returned to her home from an evening of church services, when she was startled by an intruder. She caught the man in the act of robbing her home of the valuables. She yelled, STOP! Acts 2: 38 the burglar stopped in his tracks. The woman calmly called the police and explained to them what she had done to stop the burglar. As the officer cuffed the man to take him in, he asked the burglar, "Why did you just stand there?" All the lady did was, yell a scripture at you. "Scripture," replied the burglar, "She said she had an Axe and two 38's!" To think the message in scripture is: Repent and be baptized, in the name of Jesus Christ, for the remission of sins. Acts 2: 38

MY GERMAN MAN

If not now, when?
If not, here, where?
- John Addison

I remember him after all these years. When I recall him and that time, it always seems to be before Christmas each year. As you read, you'll be able to envision him much the same as I did then.

I met him while I was in the second grade. Our family was still in Enid, Oklahoma at the time. The truth is, the story began when I was an infant and tumbled off the edge of a very high curbside downtown across from the City Square. My left eye had turned inward toward my nose. And that remained through my entering the second grade, at the old Garfield Grade School, out on the east side of town.

I returned four years ago, and while there, I paid a visit to the school. I remembered the details as I walked through the hallways. I wanted for some reason to see if a memorable painting was still in place as then. And to my amazement, it was in the same location. My memory of it was of the hills and fields and blending colors, that always reminded me of the beauty of the surrounding area.

I attended school there from the second grade through the fifth grade in 1950 - 1951. I remember the kids calling me names such as, "cross-eyed" and other hurtful kid like comments. I used to come home or would break down while out on the playground due to their cruel words shouted to me. The teacher became aware of this, and brought it to the attention of all of the kids in our classroom. In some cases it helped, but what helped most, was carrying the hurts home and telling mom and dad that it had happened. They held me in their arms trying to help me understand that none of this really mattered. Their loving me as they did, doing all possible to see that I became stronger and could ignore the kids and their name calling worked.

One morning later, mother told me we were going downtown, to meet with the eye doctor.

When he came into the room, I noticed he was about as tall as my dad. He wore a white, jacket and had black wavy hair and a full black moustache. After he examined my eye he began to tell us about the way my eye could be corrected, by having and eye operation.

He went on and said, he was fairly sure the operation would cure or bring my left eye to be straight like my right eye. I still remember how mother started to cry hearing the hopeful words.

My parents were encouraged and made arrangements for my operation.

That Sunday they took me to the hospital for my stay. The nurses took us to my room. One nurse told us another boy was in the room already. He was very sick. I sensed due to the total quiet in the room, the lights being dimmed, no one visiting him, not his mother or dad, absolute stillness. He didn't make a move, as the nurse asked me to get out of my clothes and get into my pajamas. My folks remained until I got in bed. They gave me a big hug and kiss and told me they would be back in the morning before time for my operation.

As they left, I felt so lonely and jumped out of my bed and ran over to the window, and looked down to watch them look up to my room. I stood there and cried my eyes out. They could tell I was very upset and came back into the hospital to make different arrangements for me.

Days later we were told the little boy had died.

The nurse told me the room I was going in had an older man who would be there for my stay.

He was awake and sounded like he knew I was about to join him. I heard him rustle in his bed, but I couldn't see him, as he was hidden behind a curtain.

He gave me a warm welcome and began cheering me up, kidding me and before I knew it, we were laughing together.

My folks started to leave to go home, and as they walked out of the room, the old man and I were jabbering back and forth with each other. We talked and laughed until it was time for me to go to sleep.

Mother was there the next morning as she had promised. She told me dad was working, and thinking, and praying about me and the operation.

My roommate tried to help me not to worry about my operation. Before I knew it, the nurses said, "It's time for you to come with us." "Now remember you're going to be all right and I'll be right here when you come back."

When I awoke, I was in the dark, but I could hear my friend say quietly, "Everything is going to be OK. Don't be scared being in the dark. They put the bandages over your eyes so you can heal", and added, "What you have to do is, don't scratch or try to touch the bandages or the patches on your eyes." Mother and the doctor came in to make sure I was settled, and she stayed until I went to sleep.

When I woke up I heard my roommate say, "Well, I see you finally woke up. You've been sleeping a long time."

While he and I talked and laughed at his stories, I remained in the dark. He had become my friend!

The next day he said, "I'm going to teach you how to speak German." He talked to me, in new words I had never heard before. Afterwards, he asked me to repeat him saying as best as I could the same words, which led him to also teach me to sing in German.

It wasn't that long and it would be Christmas! So, he started to sing "Olde Tatembaum". I kind of recognized it, but it sounded different. And sure enough, he helped me to learn the whole song in German.

Several mornings later, the doctor came and told me he was going to take the outside bandages off my eyes. My friend and I were excited when he began to unravel bandages, from my eyes, but I was still in the dark.

It would be two more days before they could remove the patches.

Shortly afterwards the doctor came and said, "We're going to take the patches off your eyes, but keep your eyes closed until I tell you to open them slowly, so you can adjust to the light."

"My German Man" kept cheering me on the entire time. The doctor peeled each, patch, first my right eye, then my left eye. I did what he had told me. The light was brighter than I expected. Soon afterwards I was able to see again. And you know what, I didn't have to be in the dark any more, and worry about keeping my hands off the bandages either.

Until now, I hadn't even seen my friend, "The German Man". When I turned my head, I saw him for the first time. He was older than my dad and had a gray-whitish full beard, rumpled hair, crinkled lines in his tanned cheeks, and wore his glasses that slid down to the top of his nose, sitting up snuggled on his pillows. He winked and seemed to raise his voice so it was louder than before.

My doctor told me I was going to get to go home the next day. The last night, we sang, "Olde Tatembaum", which I still sing every year at Christmas. He told me he would miss me as I had been a good roommate for him.

The next morning I went over and gave him a big hug and he hugged me back. He said, "Now be good and keep singing." As we left, I looked back at him and we both winked at each other.

It wasn't that long afterwards and mother took me down to get my first glasses. You see, the operation wasn't quite enough, but the glasses were all I needed to keep my left eye from closing in from thereon.

Mother told me I had twenty-eight stitches in the corners of my left eye and by looking in the mirror I could see them. I remembered the doctor said they were to hold my eye muscles tight, keeping my eye from turning inward as before.

When I returned to school, I told the kids about my roommate, and how I was in the dark during those days and nights.

I have never forgotten "My German Man". Every time I hear "Olde Tatembaum during the Christmas brings it all back. It was frightening, yet a wonderful time and place to heal in ways I wouldn't have imagined.

Another thing, the kids didn't call me "cross-eyed" anymore, they kidded me now and called me "four-eyes" and we all laughed.

THE MYSTERIOUS BLUE LIGHT OF MT. SHASTA

We don't see things as they are.
We, see things as we are.
Anais Nin

Mt. Shasta has long been rumored to be a place of great mystery. It is the stuff of legend. There have been books written about strange inhabitants that will sometimes wander out of the woods dressed in strange clothing that buy from the local merchants and pay in pure gold. The Indians of the area believe that the mountain is sacred, and there are many myths passed down from their descendants of strange people associated with the mountain, that appear and disappear mysteriously. Some believe that the mountain is hollow - the descendants of the lost continent of Atlantis reside there protecting their secret technology and sacred writings.

The following is a story related to me by my father. He was working as a wildlife biologist during the summer in 1990, on the southern slopes of Mt. Shasta, spending the summer conducting surveys for owls for the U. S. Forest Service. He was working alone along a little used fire road during one very hot period in July. After an early dinner, he started out into the field to begin his surveys. The day before, he had laid out call points from which he would systematically call for owls according to a pre-determined protocol. One of these call points looked over a flat pine covered plain that stretched for miles to the south. It was a beautiful spot, on a moonlight night, with the air so still you could hear your own heart beat. The country had a long and rich history with settlers, the U. S.

Calvary and the eternal conflicts, the opening of the west always brought to those early inhabitants. At near by Fort Crook, in the 1859's a young Calvary Sergeant named John Feilner, would often collect biological specimens to pass the time of an often boring posting and send the specimens back to the fledgling Smithsonian Institution in Washington, D. C. One of these specimens was an owl that had never been seen in North America. Sergeant Feilner, often spent several nights around the fort collecting owls. In his day, people often did not do anything at night, because they had nothing to illuminate the darkness other than a lantern.

The thought of Sergeant Feilner and his lantern was on my father's mind as he left camp and started for his call points on that warm July night. The acoustics of the area was particularly eerie. The whole area was honeycombed by lava tubes from a long history of volcanic eruptions; the volcanic soils seemed to amplify the peculiar behavior of sound. At times people talking a mile away could be heard clearly leaving you thinking they were standing next to you.

One of the call points was high on a spur ridge that my father could drive to in his truck. The protocol required calling and listening for an owl response for ten minutes at each call point. During the first night of calling, my father happened to glance down into the trees below the high ridge, and saw what looked like a blue light in the trees. With his binoculars, he could see that is was indeed a blue light of the type often used by railroad men, to signal the approach of a train. The peculiar thing about the light was, it appeared to move very slowly at about the speed of someone walking. My father confirmed it with his compass. At the time he was puzzled, but did not think more of it and he moved on to his other call points for the rest of the night.

The following night; the routine started over again, and my father again called the same call point. To his surprise, the strange blue light was again in the same location moving ever so slowly, swinging from side-to-side. Now, he was really struck by this odd event' he took out his compass and took a reading on the spot, where the light was moving and wrote down the direction in his notebook. At the next call point, about a mile to the north, he found himself in a small grassy arroyo below the ridge, where he had seen the blue light. During his time at this call point he suddenly felt a strange cold chill behind him. He had the distinct feeling that someone was standing behind him. But this was absurd, he was in the middle of the forest, miles from anyone on a moonlight night. Who else might be around? Just then he spun around to see if his concerns were correct, but there was no one there. The sensation did not go away. He had the distinct perception that he was being watched. It was an unnerving ghost-like experience that he could not get out of his mind the rest of the night. My father has spent years in the woods at night and is not easily frightened by anything alive or dead, so whatever it was, it had to be powerful.

The very next morning my father went back to the ridge top call point, where he had seen the blue light the night before. He took out his compass and dialed in the reading and looked with the aid of his binoculars, where the compass pointed. The trees were sparse, and there was a rather expansive stretch of grass beneath the trees, now brown from the summer heat. He could see nothing with the binoculars, so he got into his truck and drove to the area, where the compass pointed from the ridge top. The strange thing was that he found absolutely nothing, to indicate that there had been anyone there the night before. There were no tracks (my father is a good tracker), no tracks, no depressions in the grass indicating a tent had been pitched, no evidence that anyone had been anywhere near the spot, where the light had been seen. The blue light now took on a strange and mysterious aurora. What was this blue light? Where did it come from and what or who was behind it? Was there a connection to the strange cold feel that was in his bones that pressed against his spine? These questions were rolling around in my father's mind the following night as he prepared to make his last round of calling in this area.

He found himself at the ridge top call point on the third night and again he saw the strange blue light slowly moving side-to-side through the woods. What was the source of the light? Who was carrying the blue light? Who or what was behind my father that night in the arroyo that made him so cold and nervous?

Unfortunately, none of these questions were ever answered. But wile doing some research for this story, I found an entry in my father's noted dated April 16, 1990, about Sergeant Feilner. Was the source of the blue light the ghost of Sergeant Feilner wandering around the woods in search of owls? Did father's interest in owls provide some kind of other world kinship with my father 130 years later? No one really knows what the mysterious blue light was or what it meant. We will have to leave it, as one of the a multitude of mysteries that surround the strange land of Mt. Shasta.

By - Danielle Winter, who wrote this for: her English class of - December 17, 2002

BROTHER OF ARMS

My life, is what my, thoughts make,
of it.

Many of us have discovered interested war stories sorting through one's deceased belongings. I was stunned at the discovery. I found it was the most important piece of parchment I could have detected.

The article read as follows: Oregonian Journal of Portland, Oregon SUNDAY AUGUST 6, 1950 – HARBOR LIGHTS – "LARRY BATES of Milwaukie thought there was something familiar about a ship which was loading cargo in the Portland harbor, last week. Driving past terminal No. 1, Bates saw the Saginaw Victory, American-Hawaiian Steamship company vessel during World Was II, now in the inter-coastal trade.

Further investigation revealed it was the ship he had signed on as a crew member in February 1945, shortly after the vessel had been completed in Portland.

On her maiden voyage, the Saginaw participated in the invasion of Okinawa. Bates recalls the ship remained in the area for 15 days, went through some 30 air raids without major damage, and was credited with shooting down, two, Japanese, planes. The vessel was loaded with TNT and other explosives.

After pulling away from the mission, the Saginaw happened to be accidentally rammed, by another Victory ship. She continued on to Manis Island in the Admiralty group, for repairs to a gaping hole in her side."

The piece of history was nearly lost. It signified how my stepfather all of those years later, came in my life, but how he didn't or couldn't tell more of his voyages through the years. He was another Hero of Old Glory. He passed from us nearing eleven years ago, dying of asbestos pneumonia caused from the bowels of all of those ships he sailed on. At first he enlisted in the U.S. Army training at Camp Murray – across from Ft. Lewis, Washington and later became a member of the U.S. Merchant Marines. He spent his years as a member of the Black Gang, working in the engine rooms of countless vessels including the Saginaw.

I was stunned at the finding and was more proud of his service to our country than before. Those of the merchant marines were vitally important for all of our military and should have not been forgotten as to how they too participated in seeing to the needed supplies being shipped so our guys and gals could win the war as they did.

I was absolutely stunned when reading: THE WAR BY – Geoffrey C. Ward and Ken Burns and turned while reading farther in the book to the section pertaining to all that happened in the Philippines, to find on Page 344 a large photo, to be startled and know without any question, I was looking at Larry Bates. How you say? Call it a gift – where I have always been able to catalog as such, position, posture, gesture, way of turning the head, not to mention physical characteristics and know nearly every time, that I have been looking at, and in this case, even though it was years before actually coming to know him as my stepfather, it was him. Talk about irony!

A LONG DARK LINE PASSED THIS WAY LAST NIGHT

A long dark line passed through my dreams last night. Their heads held down by the silence of sacrifice. Along the way they passed through the fields of Gettysburg, the plains of Flanders, the beaches of Normandy, the black sand of Iwo Jima, and the frozen ground at Chosin.

They only stopped for awhile to say, "Don't forget us, because more will come this way."

A long dark line passed this way last night.

They spread white flowers along the way to say, "We have each given a drop of destiny that you will need to feed your children. Don't forget us along the way."

The line crossed a long dark horizon that seemed so very far away.

But they stopped long enough to say, "More will pass this way; leave a white flower to help us find our way."

ONE GIRL'S MUSICAL DEBUT

Allow me to be a blessing to you

While working, I walked into a, chiropractors, office and met the receptionist Ann Herring. It seemed we were meant to meet. As we talked, I gathered enough information and knew I had to write her story.

I asked if I could interview her and she agreed. In fact, she was very enthusiastic about my interest. Shortly afterwards we met for the interview. I had her meet me for pizza. Her warmth was evident. Ann Herring conveys a fresh vitality with a glow in her smile and a fullness of life within.

We munched on our pizza while I began to ask key questions. The first thing she told me was how she had "grown up on stage."

Ann showed me a coveted scrapbook kept by her mother. When reviewing a collection of clippings and photos of her father's life, I was drawn even more.

The account begins with her dad and her mother. They were well known, particularly her dad. He was a figurehead in the world of folk music. He practiced, taught, previewed through concerts and recorded. Merrit Herring was one of the leaders in the world of this favored music.

Ann Herring grew up on stage. Ann's mother was a practicing violinist, her dad a guitarist who sang for audiences throughout ht San Francisco Bay Area. They always took Ann with them. Not only did she grow up on stage, but it was in the company of innovators in the world of folk music.

Her dad, Merritt Herring was a great part of this movement. He wasn't only playing his guitar before audiences at the University of California, Berkeley. This was during the years from 1959 – into the sixties, during the Haight-Ashbury years in San Francisco. I thought as Ann unwound bits and pieces of the story, how my fellow students and I across the bay in San Rafael, California graduated in 1959. Their work wasn't only at UC Berkeley; it was at festivals in Marin County, at The College of Marin, in Sacramento, Davis, San Francisco, and on to Jackson Hole, Wyoming.

All of these artists were in their twenties then. For example, Pete Seeger was twenty-six. I thought of the recent PBS broadcast of his work he carried to the American public through the years. Merritt "gave a song something of himself," which became Ann's aim from the start. Like Ann, her dad sang "with a melodious voice, a clear style." It's no surprise to hear Ann's voice has the same quality today. Her dad sang Celtic song of the European tradition, hobo songs that sounded similar to Burl Ives. That was how they thought of him then. These were the years of our dancing into the summer nights week after week at the Rose Bowl in San Anselmo, California, beneath the lights hanging in the grove of oak trees. Somehow thinking back, I still hear the strumming of all of them, sharing their folk music.

Others developing and performing with Merritt were: Jean Ritchie, Shirley Collins, Mance Lipscomb, and Joan Baez. As his career unveiled itself, along came others as Alice Stuart, Count Basie, and Fred McDowell – blues man of that time. And if that wasn't enough, Merritt recorded on the Arhoolie Records label. He was viewed "with a boyish look, much the same as Bob Kennedy."

As you can see her life was more than the debuts, it included her getting to travel at an early age. Keep in mind it all began as the tiny girl looking at her dad's face.

Like Ann all of our lives are journeys.

Ann has accomplished more in her years than most could ever believe or think of achieving. Yet, she wanted me to know it came because of the love and experiences her parents provided.

An opportunity came when she was asked to travel throughout the country and play with Buddy Rich's Band. She was sixteen then. She became immersed in the business and never turned back. She was singing, performing, playing the guitar, writing and composing music, recording her songs and working with leading groups. And Ann went on to be on stage in Nashville.

In 1994 while in Nashville, she received "Song Writer, of The, Year;" the piece was "Keep on Rolling."

First, the road work which included her singing, introducing Johnny Cash, Emmie Lou Harris, Patty Loveless, the Oak Ridge Boys, Cathy Mattea, her dear friend to this day. She continued all of this until she was thirty-six.

What impressed me was that all of this came in her early years. She received a scholarship in music at Cabrillo College. A major deal she told me about included music she composed, and played and sang.

She paused, took another sip, looked up and said, "The neatest moment in my life was meeting Bill Monroe." That was the time "Running On the Wind" came for her to produce her CD.

Ann's life was then composed of working with her own jazz combo, big band work, singing in a contest in San Jose, California, working with Joni Mitchell, meeting and working with Vince Gill in his early days. Nothing could compare to her background. As I, listened and took notes furiously to keep up with her enthusiasm, I knew it all came from her parent's without question.

I found Ann slight of size, tall and willowy, and unpretentious. Her words flowed with her passions that shaped her story. I had found a true friend. Today, she is performing by working the fairs in the Northwest, playing with one of the regional groups, The Wailers.

I wasn't surprised to hear, "I'm having the most wonderful time now in my life. Like dad, I'm teaching guitar. I already have forty-five students." She is currently working at this and at the same time, like all artists, having to work a second job. I, know, the truth though. She is able to share her talent and skill with others who are aspiring as she did all those years ago. Who's to say, one will find he or she is about to debut on a stage of his own. When they think back on their lives, they will always remember the person that made success possible for them as well. When asked, who, was it, they will say with special thanks, "Her name is Ann Herring. She has done as her parents. She has given of herself and her music to me and so many others."

QUESTIONS PAID OFF FOR HER

Sometimes if you want to see a change for the Better, you have to, take, things, into your own hands.
- Clint Eastwood

When I discovered this story, I knew immediately it had to be in this book. It is far more than another story of one more" Hero of Old Glory." The writer was one young seventh grader, that was studying World War II, and to have a clearer understanding of a part of that war, that time in history, she did the following: Emily thought, the best way to gain and come to know far more than her peers, was to inquire as to the involvement of her uncle, who did more than serve his country.

Emily returned home and began to start her research –to draw information of her uncle, a bomber pilot, who flew Liberator Bombers.

This is considerably more than her story, it, is the very book that she wrote By doing this, she became extremely familiar of one very, important, member of her family.

To do this justice, I am including all of her work. As I read and became familiar as to her work, it brought me to reflect, to what I assigned to my students, of yesterday, nothing, of this caliber.

DEDICATION

This book is dedicated to Anthony Pakos. I want to thank him, for sending me money from the different countries he went to, and the medals that he gave me. This is also dedicated to all of the men and women, who have risked their lives for our country. God bless you all.

Chapter One

"BEFORE THE WAR"

Anthony Pakos was born in Loraine, Ohio on June 16, 1916.. There, he lived with his mother, father, eight brothers, and three-sisters. When he finished school, he went to work as a manager, at the Loraine Crane Company. While there, he, built cranes, and other large equipment. In 1942 when he was twenty four he enlisted in the Army Air Force. He had the courage to stand up, for what was right for the world and was ready to serve his country in war.

He enlisted so that he would not have to be drafted in the Army or Navy. When he enlisted, he said he wanted to be a bombardier. He wanted to be a hero for his country; however, knew that he might not survive, but decided to take the risk. His heroism proved to be very strong with his effort to join the war. He was sent to California for training.

In California, the training was very hard. When he first got there he was assigned a tent and given military clothing, and as all recruits sent all of his (civilian clothes and effects) home, spent hours daily doing physical training, as needed to get back in shape, which included running three miles a day. The remainder of the day was spent in the classroom. An emphasis was mathematics leading to all that his career field entailed. The fellow recruits of varying fields had been away from school for years, making all challenging for them.

Anthony and fellow Airmen found their relaxation came by: attending chapel call, catching the latest motion picture on base –grabbing moments from the studies. Upon training being accomplished he was assigned, to head for Arizona for more advanced training among the other nine men for far more than they originally planned.

And from there to New Mexico, where he told me he was not pleased, with the air-base, he was assigned to, due to it being located in a desert. All that was there were two restaurants, one movie theatre. Boring! But, the morale was excellent among the men that now were starting to look to facing combat in the war zone ahead.

He told me his interchange from one state to another was the same as the slide-rule, they had to use in their training. Now back to Arizona where he completed his training. Then, they left for Africa. It was 1943, when they arrived to do their part in the war. The first was flying in B-24 bombers and finally when thinking back, he was dropping the bombs.

Anthony revealed bravery, courage needed to reveal even stronger results in the battle ahead. Africa was where the real fight had already begun.

Chapter Two

"COMBAT"

Anthony Pakos was assigned outside of Cairo, Egypt upon arriving there, he was able to see why all before had been in the desert in the states. The mission was to stop General Erwin Rommel, the German military leader for the German Army.

In February 12, 1943 he was assigned to his first bombing mission in Naples,

Italy. At the time, the Germans had many ships heading in the harbor, giving supplies to their troops in the area, shipping all to Egypt. Even though Anthony's bomb group had twelve airplanes (where normally the group would include forty-eight aircraft), one true fact was, the same for them. They were waiting, for more aircraft not only, in Africa, through Europe, and in the Pacific islands. Consequently, the results of their raids were negligible to the enemies, airplanes.

The air battles resulted with the enemy firing guns, not to forget the ack – ack – ack, with the sound of the shells exploding in mid-air.

What was hardest was their losing twelve planes to the fighter planes and knowing none of the crews within those planes lived. The results were unknown what with the darkness of the night. Problems arose but they fought on through the mission. At the end of each bomb run, was the debriefing of their results of the attack, all that they saw and what they all felt regarding the bomb runs.

Afterwards, came, the full inspection to determine the damage received to their (ships) planes. His plane was damaged far more than imagined. Four engines were knocked out. This left him amazed that not one member of the crew had been hit. They knew without question they could have been killed.

More and more they better understood all of the training before and the conditions they had faced, finding much of the same, living in tents, having to eat only leftover food from World War I (spam, canned ham, and powdered eggs). Where before they ate well, slept in beds, not make shifts, even had laundry service. No longer! The hours were beyond grueling – with more missions ahead.

He and fellow aircraft crews kept "the push" back in March – April of 1943 – for the Army Air Force was moving forward across North Africa. The bomb runs hit throughout Italy, Greece and the island of Sicily. Finally, they began to receive long needed equipment, enabling far more damage toward their bomb runs. The targets included: industrial areas in cities where war materials were manufactured and airfields for the enemy planes.

Imagine, remaining in the air for fourteen hours at a time. And the results became more and more effective, as their experience, so were the targets that were being destroyed. Throughout April, May, and June, the survival rate fortunately included little damage or loss of lives. As expected, Anthony became as his crew, more proficient.

One of the missions a piece of anti-aircraft flak (an iron piece of shell which exploded in mid-air) hit and unfortunately, their pilot was hit, but not seriously injured. Anthony learned as fellow crew members, how vital it was to wear their head gear. In his case, his position was always in thee very nose of the plane, readying to aim and gain the controls to drop the bombs, he was hit, fortunately, it bounced off, only left a dent in his helmet. Luck was with him, for had he been three feet lower he would have died, and all here would have been lost.

Mid June came with a long needed R & R (rest and recreation). They were bound for Tel Aviv in Israel. When thinking back he shared, to have the recreation, clean clothing, improved food, even comfortable beds and a long needed shower was what they needed most.

Their next station was in Libya, near Benghazi. He remained stationed there until the end of the war.

Now the mission was changing in July of 1943, upon getting instructions to begin practicing low-level bombing, an abrupt change from having dropped the payload at twenty-thousand feet, to targets fifty to one hundred feet off the ground. And the raid was destined to Ploesti.

Chapter Three

"PLOESTI"

Anthony's, crew, was now sent, to Ploesti, Romania with the aim to drop bombs over the oil fields – "Ploesti was an oil boom city at the foot of Transylvanian Alps, thirty-five miles north of Bucharest" (Dugan and Stewart 22). All before and up to the present revealed, how skilled he was as a bombardier doing more than his part in serving our country as one of the Airmen involved in World War II.

The raids on Ploesti were chosen for there were the large oil fields, which produced the fuel and oil needed for the German war effort. The U.S. Chief of Staff, General Marshall said, "That a fairly successful attack on the refineries would stagger the enemy." (Dugan, Stewart 23).

This was the first bombing mission of its kind; and the effort included the merger of England there to help with the raid. "This gave them a total of four bomb groups, which consisted of over 140-150 airplanes that were supposed to hit the target" (Pakos, Anthony).

Anthony and many other men were taken by surprise when the realized what they were up against. The alternated route was going across the Mediterranean, climbing to 25,000 feet having to skirt over the water over part of Italy, Greece, and Mt. Olympus. "They were told to fly at 100 feet because they needed to go over high obstacles in thee oil fields" (Pakos, Anthony). These included chimneys of the cranking plants and the boilers that created steam needed to refine the oil. But the finding was that, the Germans had been alerted to their arrival, awaiting the fleet with ground guns and airplanes to down the encroaching bombers. And to top it, there was a mix up in the flying pattern and some of the planes flew off in the wrong direction. Result equaled confusion toward the target!

To hear this was more than Anthony's admission. He said, "because of the problem, part of the target was already in flames as his plane passed, the German fighters were shooting at them, knocking their planes down." And, continued saying, "They seem to be enjoying it!"

Unfortunately, the planes and crews that went the wrong way over the target did not make it, bringing an ineffective result toward the target. "The outcome should have been 80-90% damage, which would have shut down the refinery; we only did 50-60% damage, leaving the refinery still running."

The return flight encountered flocks of the German fighters which hit Anthony's plane severely. Fortunately, he and crew were able to return to base. All of them realized after inspection of their craft, that it was a marvel to have survived. And at the same time the result of the mission was to "lose thirty airplanes and when thinking of the nine to ten crew members of each was staggering." They were certain that none had survived, for all were unable to parachute out at one-hundred feet and left with no place to land.

All resulted in a failed mission for the refinery was not damaged enough to stop production and far too many aircraft had been downed.

Ahead were more missions and a far better result. Nightly though, Anthony and others were left with reflections of having to see their fellow Airmen lost during the battle and the destruction played over and over for all. Emily summed all of this up saying, "Even though Anthony failed this mission, he would heroically win many other battles among his fellow Airmen…this was a horrifying experience, but he got through it with courage and bravery."

Chapter Four

"GOING HOME"

Anthony Pakos received a flying cross, the second highest medal given by the Army Air Force. He said, "I would've gladly given up the medal to have seen us do a better job over the target and see a lot fewer people lost on this particular raid." And Emily added, "Being willing to give up his medal proves that he is a hero."

After receiving the honor, others were able to return homeward before. In the meantime, another mission came to bomb Sicily, Messina, and Naples because they found out that the Allies were going to invade Sicily from Africa, they wanted to totally disrupt the communication abilities. What was seen from his prime position in the nose of his plane observing the whole invasion fleet coming from North Africa to Sicily. This time the protective arm flew with them, fighter planes for the mission.

Upon returning to their base, the finding was the invasion of Sicily was going down on the ground. In the meantime, the bombing raids continued in Italy. After, the last bombing mission in Naples, he received the third highest medal, the Air Medal for great heroism.

His twenty-fifth mission, he successfully bombed a harbor on the other side of Italy. The result was that they had hit a large ship and sunk it. Not only the, ship the result was total destruction by all of the bombs. All of this brought only the loss of two planes, crew members being able to parachute out, which led them to spend the duration of the war in, prisoner camps. And upon returning to the base when he heard, "You're going home pack right away, for your flight returns tomorrow."

Talk about overjoyed! He wanted me to know, "I'm sure I probably broke down and cried because this was such a sudden change. All of a sudden I'm going back to the peaceful, beautiful United States of America to see my family and my friends." And talk about dispatch, it didn't matter to him if all he had was his tooth brush.

Before returning to the states, first it was to Cairo, Egypt the very next day, to a very fancy hotel, a few days for needed R & R before departure for the last flight to home.

Two days later he landed in Miami, Florida and continued to Cleveland, Ohio., And when finding these words, this reminded me of what I had heard years later, but in Anthony's case he heard, "He didn't know if there was a plane going to Ohio."

In Anthony's case he made sure the attendants knew he had just returned from North Africa after his last bombing mission. The clerk said, "He didn't know he was a combat veteran, because you weren't wearing your medal on your uniform." Why – because it was far too hot in Cairo.

The next morning he was on his way to Georgia, then on to Washington D.C. And if you can imagine, he heard from the M.P.'s (Military Policemen) "You need to be more presentable." And Anthony replied, "I have been in Africa on a bombing mission and these are the only clothes I have." The M.P. gave him a tie. And Anthony asked, "Where could he get a flight to Cleveland."

It was hard for Anthony to believe or think his war story was over, ahead was his new life which had just begun.

Emily said with repetition that, "Anthony proved his heroism in World War II by having the courage and strength to keep going, never giving up, even when he was at the worst of times. Because of his bravery, he showed he was a hero."

This story came from the grand daughter of dear friends of mine, by, Emily A. Pool in her seventh grade class – today she is attending college locally.

Works Cited

Dugan, James, Stewart, Carroll. Ploesti. New York: Random House Inc. 1962

"Loraine Flier Describes Crushing Raid on Axis." Loraine Journal. August 20, 1943

"Loraine Veteran of Air War Now Teaching Fliers.," Loraine Journal November 26, 1943

Newby, Leroy. Target Ploesti View From a Bobsight. New York: Presdo Press. 1983

Pakos, Anthony. Personal Interview, January 12w, 2001

Pakos, Dick. Personal Interview, January 3, 2001

"Ploesti Bomber Safe in Spite of Jinx Day Crash." Loraine Journal.

Popescu, Juilian. Romania. New York: Chelsea House Publishers, 2000

"Praises Heroism of Akron Officer." Loraine Journal.

"Promoted," Loraine Sunday News.

Shubert, Lyndon. "Raid, on Ploesti." < http://www.the historynet.
com/Aviation
History/articles/2000/0300 cover.htm>   (January 16, 2001)

Team-Ploesti. {teamploesti@hotmail.com} "Ploesti" <
http://www.personal.lig.bellsouth.net/lig/v/e/vedwrds/ploesti/
>(January 16, 2001)

"Tells of Thrills, on Ploesti Raid." Loraine Journal. September

"Tidal Wave, the August 1943 Raid on Ploesti."
http://wwwairforcehistory.hq.af.mil/soi/ploesti.htm

"Yanks, and British in Relay Raids on Naples" Loraine Journal. April
6, 1943

WHERE IT CAME FROM

The future belongs to those that believes,
in the beauty, of their dreams.
Eleanor Roosevelt

I want all of you readers to know where "Chit-Chat-Café" came from.

My mother was working as a waitress at my very favorite spot then; it was the "Chit-Chat-Café" in my hometown of Enid, Oklahoma.

The outside was painted clean white; all of the trim was in red, including the painted on sign on the outside siding, to welcome one and all to the "Chit-Chat-Café". There were other signs such as the one hung in the window of the door that signified this spot was open. Two of those neon signs were hanging in the window up high, not taking the view from those inside, saying they carried Pepsi, "More Bounce to the Ounce." They had ice-cream delights to. When you walked in the layout was shaped like an L. The counter was directly in front of you.

You either saw people licking their lips as they were walking outside or heard them rave about their hamburger, fries and milk shake. Behind the counter, you could look in the kitchen and hear and see those sizzling meals about to be served. The waitresses were so special, you knew they were friends by the way they kept up such a friendly chat with all. They were immaculate in their frock like dresses and aprons. Each kept their pencil stuck in their hair or their aprons to take down every order. Even as you sat, you would hear this constant

"Chit-Chat" coming from the kitchen with, "Orders Up", whether it was my mother or one of the other waitresses, they would pick up those platters with the ease of a juggler of hot plates. The meals were carried and delivered to each of the tables. They asked if there was anything else you needed, maybe coffee or cream.

Had you been looking at those in the booths or the whole place, you would have sworn that famous painter, Norman Rockwell had been there.

The "Chit-Chat-Café" was like an extended family for me. I wanted to spend as much time there with mother as possible. She was working to keep us together as a family. This was my way of saying my deep heartfelt thanks to her. Everything was warm and welcome there. It was good for a tune on the jukebox. One tune was a favorite and always reminded me of my mother and all of her regulars, "The Tennessee Waltz."

You got the very best view at the front counter, which overlooked all of the booths and tables. Why, there's the Enid Chief of Police, who became my friend, seeing that I had an old Smith and Wesson 38 revolver, with the firing pin severed off to be safe. He was a tall man who wore a moustache and you could tell he had plenty of experience over the years, the roadmap was all over his face, and even showed in his hands stirring his coffee., He would sit down and be visiting my mother and in came the Fire Chief. You knew they enjoyed joshin' each other. They kidded mother and asked, "What the special this morning was for breakfast" in a jocular way.

The clothier and his staff entered and took their booth up by the window looking out on the City-Square. Mother shared, they stood out because they wore the best in fashion. The owner of their store seemed to like his pancakes.

Other business people came in and sat greeting all within and ordered their morning coffee. A typical sound that seemed to come from one and all was, "Ah," after sipping their coffee.

The Police Chief got up and went over to the counter and paid his bill all the time talking with the Fire Chief as they returned to their offices.

Regulars came as the owner of the music store. I wouldn't ever have imagined the day would come in the future, that I would be playing a sousaphone, like the one he had in the window of his store.

Ladies came and had their drinks, breakfast or lunch, would get their mirrors out and make sure their lipstick was just right, their hair in place before going back to their office on the City-Square. They clicked out in their pretty dresses, high heeled shoes, with that definite line showing on the back of their legs, as they walked away.

The owner and his wife came out of the kitchen to greet those already there for the morning. That was how every day went. The door kept swinging all day until closing at night.

I made my last trip home after all of those years while away. The first place I asked to see was the "Chit-Chat-Café." I found it wasn't there. A new Bank was at that location. That place, and those people, have been present in my memories ever since.

THEN THERE WAS JON

The, most important thing, about
Goals, is, having one.
Geoffrey F. Abert

Thinking of Jon Winter, takes me back to days long ago. He has always been there for me. He was a star halfback; and played the flute in the orchestra; I was in the band playing the tuba, which gave us something we had in common from the start.

He was not over six feet tall, had a full head of hair, suave; a guy that somehow had little difficulty attracting girls in our class or community. He wore a cord coat with khaki pants, and walked with assurance; he drove the latest model Plymouth; it was later that I found his dad owned an automobile agency. He was able to get jobs with the same ease, and didn't have to pound the pavement to find employment as I did, "The New Kid in Town."

Jon saved my butt! I was a transfer student who joined my family in San Rafael, the summer of 1958. This enabled my stepfather to ship out of San Francisco, and surrounding ports as a merchant marine.

What a change. One guy came at the best time of all, Jon Winter. He must have known the toughness of trying to fit in that year, in town and at school. We went everywhere together, including his interests in birding on weekends; he introduced me to Johnny Mathis' recordings and other forms of jazz. What was prominent in my memory was it didn't matter whether others understood what he did.

With spring came the track and field turnouts. I remember how he told me about top runners, how they had taught him a more effective way to run. He shared, "You'll run even more smoothly, if you raise each leg, cross it in front and let your hips fall or sag, you know, how women walk, point your toe as you come down." As I tried this, I felt, a smoothness a, "swing of the hips."

Even though he spoke softly, words were not lost in any conversation. His knowledge of trivia amazed me, and does to this day, trivia about leading athletes and their achievements that stagger the mind. When we listened to Johnny Mathis, he told me of Mathis' record as a high jumper in high school while in San Francisco. Jon composed his own music, and beat rhythms on his congo and bongo drums.

I remember how we cruised across the Richmond-San Rafael-Bridge in his new Plymouth, sitting back smoking our Kent cigarettes, not inhaling, but knowing we had that look of "cool" as we merged into the East Bay world of jazz. We listened to jazz groups, and enjoyed at the same time, fresh hot stew in one quaint little spot, where we had the opportunity to hear Jerry Mulligan along with more jazz artists. The Black Hawk in San Francisco was another jazz stop for us. Then we'd stop on the waterfront, for a bite of crab and sour dough bread before heading back to San Rafael.

He told me later, his dad had interest in him as long as he was in sports. When he blew his knees out, while playing football and had his scholarship to the University of Oregon which was lost, their relationship became a thing of the past. It saddened me to hear this. To think, that his, dad, wasn't interested, in his study of birds, gaining the scholarly background as a biologist, not to mention, his interest in music. I know that was a loss for him too. However, I knew he was proud of his father, for he knew all his father had accomplished, even though Jon was a youngster, when his dad enlisted in World War II, and he was gone for three to four years training and serving throughout Europe.

Jon had his father's records of how he had earned four major battle stars as an Army Major at Normandy, the Battle of the Bulge, and

France, for the invasion of Germany, as one of the "Greatest Generation." Granted, Jon, his brother and mother did as all of the families then, waited and hoped and prayed for his safe return. Upon his return, his father did as vast numbers of the men and women coming home, went into business beginning his professional career in the automotive and tire business in Butte, Montana. After the war, they moved to California and settled in San Francisco, later to San Rafael.

His mother was the one that appreciated Jon's many qualities.

Have you ever heard of a young boy or girl, who kept a log of his or her life year to year? Jon did. That list was like the ones any birder might keep of his sightings. He never revealed any of it to convey he was better than me or anyone else. He always made a point of letting each person be an individual.

We planned to travel throughout Europe after graduation. To earn money he worked as a forest fire lookout in the Willamette National Forest in Oregon. I worked as a dock man, loading delivery trucks and had my own milk route. Due to changes, though, I couldn't match the sum needed. To this day, he still yearns to make that trip. Who's to say, that we still may make that sojourn.

As is true, we separated from one another. I enlisted into the U.S. Air Force, he drifted on to college. After his departure from football came his desire to study music in New York City. Instead, he studied with jazz artists playing in the "Big Apple."

When I asked whether he had continued with the flute, it was a sad note to hear, "I gave it up when someone stole my instruments."

After finding each other via Classmates Reunion, many years later my wife and I made plans to sail on the ferry crossing San Francisco Bay to the Larkspur Landing in Marin County. Jon and I immediately recognized each other. The hugs followed as if to grasp hold of more than each other, truthfully, to grab hold of every one of those years. Misty eyes were evident. Another good friend, Mike Marcley came for our reunion as well.

Introductions were passed one to the other, as they hadn't met my wife. Five hours later it was time to return to our homes, ours with our son and his wife in Tracy, California and they headed home to Santa Rosa to the north.

Meeting them was as though no time had passed at all since seeing them last in 1961. The evidence of time passing was less hair, a slower walk, the same caring loving Jon and Mike of yesterday. Jon was clad in blue jeans, a blue and red plaid shirt, his ball cap tipped back on his head; it became evident he didn't want to take his hat off. He slipped his cap off showing wisps of hair and a shiny balding head, just like me. But he was even more at ease, far more relaxed than years before. Our conversation continued, as if to cover all of the lost miles we had between us through the years. It wasn't a surprise to me that he still had a keen knowledge of the trivia. All and all he was the same Jon I had known.

We realized that a kind of richness was ours that carried across the years, and miles to this very day.

He has friends across the country which he talks about from time to time. They are leading birders, biologists, with whom he did research as far away as Antarctica, later to return to become a tour guide. Then on to graduate school – to San Francisco State University for graduate work in ecology, where he completed his thesis, on the Great Gray Owl – and gained his Master's Degree.

His knees kept him from joining or being drafted into the military or having to serve in Vietnam.

That's not all. After looking at what he referred to as, Life Notes and Personal Chronology, WHO'S WHO In California, a glimpse of his photo while at San Rafael High the year of 1958 – 1959, looking at another group photo of him, with those in New York, who were making a reputation in the jazz circles, looking one more time at the photos taken while at the Larkspur Landing; and reading emails that we had sent back and forth to each other, I knew there was more to say.

He added, "I wouldn't have looked at me quite the way you have, but I believe what you wrote is fine." Always, that, gracious, "reach-out" spirit of his.

To read his notes, I found he raised a Flammulated Owl, "that I found had fallen on the ground," eventually he went down to the area where he discovered a whole population of this species. They were considered rare at the time. Little was known about them. Since that time, a great deal has been learned. He continued saying, "I would just go down there, and work with the birds at night, until I got a 'feel' for what they were doing and learned about the behavior," He continued saying, "I still work on owls, although, it's now for money and not fun, but my work on the Great Gray Owl was a passion and my feelings for the bird have not changed all these years. And, resumed, "Those were the best years, of my, life."

To know Jon deeper meant you had to realize he did so much more than dabble.

How he became such a jazz enthusiast was a story of its own. Another friend cared enough to introduce him to a recording by Bud Shank and a selection called Lotus Bud hooked him. Few of us find that certain something that hooks us.

Many of us could say the following: "I studied by watching and learning." He went on to tell me, "I never looked back."

So much music was within him. He could play drums and found, he was good at Latin Rhythms…in fact drums seemed to be easy for him. The flute took considerably more work. Upon arriving in New York City, he met a group called, Jazz Composers Guild, that played dramatic and avant garde music at the time. There, he worked with the Free Form Improvision Ensemble (as you can see in the photo included) from a 1964 issue of Downbeat Magazine.

Others that left their mark on him happened to be: the musician Ornette Coleman, and Bill Dixon, playwright Paddy Chayesfsky, poet Leroi Jones, and poet Alan Ginsberg. He met the painter Hans Hoffman, sculptor Alexander Calder, Leonard Bernstein, even the composer Aaron Copeland, and jazz pianist Valdo Williams. Williams told him under a rather dim street lamp in Greenwich Village, "A true artist is only an observer of his own flow of consciousness." He went on and added, "If you do anything to impede that flow, you cease to be an artist." That moment brought Jon to think of what the composer Igor Stravinsky said, "I am just the vessel which through the music flows."

He was now marked without question and through all that followed.

What was to flow as the notes or the score of his life, would be more work at the lookouts, travels, realizing what came to him as a child of having such a fascination of birds, nature, the out of doors, would become the magnet that would continually attract him from thereon.

Jon put himself through college working on fire lookouts on the Tahoe National Forest in California. He was nearly robbed by "banditos" while in Mexico. Like many others, he was drawn to the culture of the hippies of San Francisco to the Haight-Ashbury scene in the 1960's.

Then, he continued to Bolinas to the Point Reyes Bird Observatory. But to see him among his peers, there was a new look, of one of the team, standing in the photo, not so suave now, in the weathered kind of look, with jeans, shirt for more warmth, a leader among all of the others in the photo. Now his hairline was with long side burns, no beard, and a field hat. I could tell he was definitely one that had come to realize his true calling, the caring for the wildlife of yesterday and to the present day.

He traveled to South America for further studies, to Arizona, Colorado, Utah, South Dakota, and Minnesota. Finally, he settled to study martial arts and earned his 3rd Degree Black Belt in Korean Tae Kwon Do and Arnis – Philippine stick fighting and to become an instructor.

Years of such adventures were his. He and his wife, Christine and two daughters live in Santa Rosa, California.

He told me how he, "Worked out of a little cabin in a very large meadow system near Yosemite National Park. Some of the best years and hardest of my life were spent at that cabin (Ackerson Meadow) working on owls…I have a long history with that place at all times of the year."

He continues to work in private industry since 1991. He's become a consultant in the Wildlife Biology overall. He concluded saying, "Not a very interesting life but it is a living."

I thought back about how Jon had become and would always be the finest friend in my lifetime, definitely, far more like a brother, one of the Band of Brothers. It was a privilege to write his complete portrayal, the way it needed to be to reveal to you the reader, a full look at this guy, I had come to love and respect, as long ago as our first years together up to this very time in our lives.

Ann Herring
From: One Girl's Musical Debut

Joe Zelazny
From: Betty Grable and Alice Faye Made Me Do It

Joe Zelazny
With Wife Lorrayne
From: Betty Grable and Alice Faye Made Me Do It

Joe Zelazny
Today
From: Betty Grable and Alice Faye Made Me Do It

Sue Bledsoe
From: Search for Hometown

Danielle Winter
From: The Mysterious Blue Light of Mt. Shasta

Jon Winter
Pt. Reyes, California
Bird Observatory Staff
From: Then There Was Jon

Jon Winter
Biologist Birder
From: Then There Was Jon

Emily Pool
War Map
From: Questions Paid Off For Her

Emily Pool
From: Questions Paid Off For Her

Dorothy Guber Holmstrom
From: Ahead a Mystical Journey

Bonnie and Roger Himka
From: For Some Golf and Fishing Is Enough

Bonnie Himka
From: For Some Golf and Fishing is Enough

Dylan Cash & Papa
From: First Days Of His Life

Karina Schwartznau
JA 3 2008 Junior Olympics
From: Without a Doubt a Future Olympian

Karina Schwartznau
From: Without a Doubt a Future Olympian

Karina Schwartznau
and Libby Ludlow, Olympian
From: Without a Doubt a Future Olympian

Paul Baumgardt, Age 98
From: A Man and His Garden

REGRETFULLY, WE DENY THEM OUR ATTENTION

God has sprinkled some very faithful and very
caring souls around us, and it is indeed
a wonderful thing to make that
"rare find" to receive that,
"breath, of fresh air" in
the contest of human relationship is one just
doesn't, want, to let it go, once it is found.
Anonymous

The male gender needs to reflect more on women in our lives. They have been with us since the beginning of time. There has always been the question, as to whether they were created from man's side or not. Even though there is this to be argued over, it seems that matters not. What matters, is, they, have been there at our side for ever. Whether we want to or not, they not only are, we can count on them remaining.

The intent of this isn't, to preview women, all they have suffered, and at the same time been able to fight with grit to arrive as they have. We certainly should! To do this requires us to focus on: their being contributors in the act of pro-creation, gift givers of the finest gift any of us could ever hope for – life, itself - carrying us from the beginning, holding us, going through intensity of pain, agony, welcoming us with our first kiss, caressing us as we have grown, being ones that we can call, no matter our plight, there to cheer us, bring us to better understand moments of success and failure, companioning us as our friends; foremost, becoming our partners for our lives.

This can't continue without a brief look back.

It's meant to be a tribute, lighting of the brightest candle possible.

The way has been arduous. Imagine the journey they have taken.

"Imagine," to be the fashion plates they have had to be, no matter the place or time, to fight for their place no matter where or when, to accept the call of fighting, standing tall, having to gain rights achieved through suffrage. For becoming today's woman, a soldier, officer, in charge, means still fighting for what they face.

Today's woman leaves us to wonder, do they want to be all they insist on being. Is it primarily due to what we as man have forced, on, them? We know for the most part, it is all but impossible for any or all family units to survive, bare all we do everyday alone. No longer can women remain in the home, caring for our homes, nurturing children as they do. It takes both parties to merge into the work-a-day world; the huge question rises, that is not only why or what can be done to alter this path.

As I write, I can't do this justice without thinking back into my past, as to what I have seen. I remember two women in particular.

First, was my great grandmother, Ginny that came from Missouri marrying my Great Grandfather, Jasper, known as Poppa, both seventeen and eighteen years of age moving as they did to the prairie land of Oklahoma. Upon arriving, they tilled the land, built a Sod-Hut, and as the years continued, raised nine boys and girls and had one other come. The additional one happened to be my mother, who was raised by her grandparents from infancy, to graduating from Skeedee High School, in Skeedee, Oklahoma, a tiny little railroad town, where farming was the primary way of life. Ginny's work was as vital as Poppas, who was a railroad man for the Southern Pacific, tended the water tower and the station stop. While he was working, Ginny was busier than modern day women, washing clothes, sewing, preparing meals, cleaning, gardening, collecting eggs, nurturing children, participating in church activities, towns and school duties, most important, there to welcome and love Poppa.

I'm sure many of you may have had as I, the opportunity to see your relatives at a tender age. I vividly remember seeing her as youngster. You may have had your first pretty frock or in my case, my very first long pair of pants and a little suit when I went to see her. What I remember was the little white house located on top of the hill, at the end of the street, looking down into the bramble bush, seeing the path that Poppa took for years back and forth to the railroad station. I recall seeing this tiny little woman in her house dress walking with a bent over stoop, showing me her flower beds. I know it was a special visit, for my mother always remembered those days with this loving woman, that gave her a home from infancy Those visits weren't that often before she was gone.

Then, there was my grandmother, I saw from her visits at our home. She was away working, traveling the country for years, serving hot breakfasts, lunches, pouring coffee for the customers in cafés as a waitress. Upon joining her, she was still working over those counters, smiling, serving hot coffee and meals to those stopping for their usual. The picture was seeing her in those worn, white polished shoes, the apron soiled from the days work, having that work a day look. Yet, somehow when joining her, was this picture of how she made sure the home fires were always lighted, lunch buckets packed with a good lunch, dutifully, making sure we were wrapped and had our gloves, rubber galoshes on and snapped, our stocking hats placed on our heads, warm winter jackets zipped ready for the cold walk to school. She always had a warm welcome for us each afternoon upon return - and made sure to have a warm snack as a roll all buttered, fresh baked cookies from the oven for us with a glass of milk, and made sure we could play cribbage, some board game, or just sit and she would point out the flocks of seagulls flying in from another storm. There was always the thrill, of she, and I making sure to watch the World-Series every year without fail. Talk about a baseball fan!

The change that was taking place throughout the country of the women having to step up and fulfill the roles of the men off to war, working roles as "Rosie the Riveter," office jobs, pouring coffee over another counter. If they were able to stay home, it was a good thing for their children. Think back in your case, for I know you remember those years; and the very position that the lady, your mother, played in those days.

Children found they were holding down the fort, while their mothers worked. We didn't think anything of it.

They are more in number than the young men they attend college classes with, taking charge as to the curriculum, accepting roles of leadership, or ones that make far more money than the men in the jobs or professions they hold. Their hours aren't anything as compared to the years before. Today, we see them work outside the home, work in the home, care for the children, picking the kids up from school daily to keep them safe, becoming involved in social positions, political positions, serving on committees that help the community, church work, volunteers in hospitals, being loving women still home with hot cookies and milk for their children, there for their men, yes - still revealing how tired they are, for there always is something that has to be done. Women of today, still have to find time, energy to feed the baby, prepare microwave dinners, iron and press the men's shirts, wash the clothes, hopefully, thank the men in their homes for all they do to help out when or wherever needed.

Women now see the roles reversed, men are staying home doing similar duties, and they are working. Men have in many cases chosen to take those roles. Yet, there is that frazzled look on women's faces, but a new look and fashion. Where men made sure all was mechanically done, now, the woman is the one that takes the car to have the mechanic fix the brakes... get the tires checked or repaired, making sure all members in the family get to the appointments with the doctors, take the children out to shop, and the list goes on and on.

Through all of it, we realize how tough they really are. Now they are doctors, attorneys, truck drivers, working traffic signs at construction jobs, driving school busses, working as Assistant Professionals, pursuing opportunities through the medical fields, lunchroom cooks, helpers, police officers, dentists, hygienists, accountants, teachers, coaches, professional athletes, cooks, bakers, authors of leading books and editors, writers of books, magazines, newspapers, owners of companies, accountants to name only a few.

Foremost-giving birth, to the children! Today, models of the latest in fashion, even designers.

Now, I know, the picture has to be quite vivid, as what and where women have evolved. Talk about respect. There are no gaps! This writer takes his cap off for them every day and every where.

MANY A MILE

Our setting couldn't have been more perfect. Everyone had come to celebrate with the guest of honor! He had quite a lot to share with all. He had just retired from his position of forty – five years. Had it been any other, he would be announcing his stepping away from his company and staff members. Not him though. His position would have been perceived as, a menial, way to earn a living by some. Not me.

His training for this could be considered rather unusual though. Honestly, when he told me I could more than see how Ray, a new recruit in the U.S. Army was shipped to Fort Campbell, Kentucky to train for the artillery duties, in his case – no it wasn't fork lifts, he was becoming a tank driver. That's right - he paused and – I realized I found over a short meeting some time ago, which was terrific for it was the rounding out of his story not gained before. I believe he told me he was in training for some ten or more weeks. And afterwards, he was not only a driver inside a tank with three other crewmen, he said, "You bet it went plenty fast, some fifty-five miles an hour or more. To see ahead everything was by periscope." And he added, "We could stop those tanks, on a dime."

His story, can't but remind us, of the daily care takers of the dirty-nasty jobs throughout the country, that are ignored by immense numbers in surrounding cities, towns and bergs.

This guy sat aboard a fork lift where he had cruised what became more than a route, it was a habitual path, where he had been the master board lifter. He did more than, heft board, by, the, foot, in fact; his work was, moving wooden boxes of all dimensions. For more than years, it included being knowledgeable and able to know precisely where and why, to drop loads for all of those years. Load upon load sliding into storage slots, loads on and off truck and trailers, most importantly, doing all of the work with safety, for all working in the midst.

There were more here today than were expected, but they couldn't equate to the occasion.

Family members, some fellow employees, friends, were there to share their appreciation for more than the work, it was as though everyone could envision all of the mornings, Ray, rose to the alarm clock, shaves and showers, and nicks from the blade, not to mention numbers of varied breakfasts, vicariously, observing him leave for days, months, now years to drive to work, arrive and punch his time card, check the log to all of the days of work.

And today, everyone has come, either shook or are shaking his hand, making sure to pat him on the shoulder, or a big hug congratulating him, enjoying the company of others grabbing a drink – beer or pop, some nibbles, all on hold for the prepared lasagna, crisp garlic bread, salads and all of the trimmings for dinner. And finally, the cake with glasses to lift champagne, and the all important toast, in completing thanks, and congrats for him, and all of his love ones.

Now, to begin many seasons of traveling, the first trip he has shared will be to Mexico, where they love it so, to name only a few of his activities he has planned for all of this time.

Retirement indeed! Oh, one more thing, it has been both a pleasure, no sir, it has been my privilege to share his story with all of you fine people.

A HEAD A MYSTICAL JOURNEY

When hearing this saga, I was more than intrigued and wanted to include it among the other "Heroes of Old Glory" for it was about one member of the Army Nursing Corps. Dorothy couldn't understand why I thought her account from her would merit my wanting it in the collection of World-Wide short stories. I saw it as more than interesting – besides this is one of the primary ways women could serve at that time.

Dorothy Guber Holmstom happened to be someone that I met with other members at their weekly veteran meeting. Today she is young at spirit at ninety years of age.

She was born on June 26, 1918 in Cobban, Minnesota. I recently tried to contact her, finding her back in Minnesota; however, it seemed near impossible to convey all that was coming. I finally contacted her son; told him that due to her being hard of hearing, and said no more, for he more than understood and was very pleased that I thought enough of his mother, to want to write of all she had done, doing her part for our country then.

She told me, "Dad was a carpenter by trade, a guy that built houses, even barns. And mother as women then, a housewife who took care of all on the home front."

Rush City, Minnesota was where they moved to leading her to graduate from high school in 1936. She told me, "One key reason wasn't just that I graduated, dad was a millwright and the mill burned down July 3, 1936."

She took up archery to get the best in exercise. Dorothy proudly told me of her brother who was a school bus driver – for her classmates consisted of fifty-two students, no, it was eight-four of us. Dorothy added, "I graduated when I was eighteen. The kids always said I was going to be a nurse from day one, sure enough, it turned out they were right." The years passed, but led me to tell my parents, "If you give me fifty-dollars, I'll start nursing school." And that was when her dad and mom went east to New Jersey.

Then she told me her work began at St. Andrews Hospital in Minneapolis, Minnesota at the School of Nursing. Her class consisted of only eleven women; they were attending school together for three to four years, the program was year round. Other duties included split shifts and were involved in every aspect of nursing readying them for all ahead. Keep in mind my interview with her was sometime ago, but I do remember her telling of one place four – five of her classmates frequented, that was Jack's Restaurant, near The University of Minnesota.

From there, Dorothy had duties which consisted of: private duty, intensive care, unknown to her at the time, there were going to be shifts unlike anything she had been involved in.

"I joined the service in 1943, to be in the U. S. Army Corps of Nursing" and even more far fetched, to think her journey that I am about to share with all of you took her all the way to Iran.

She resumed saying "Dad and mom took me to the railroad station to see me off, not knowing when or even if I would see them again. I boarded a Pullman car, which was more than I had ever experienced before."

It was a troop train among all of the draftees and others that had enlisted, they all had apprehension.

She commented, "My first stop was in Chicago, Illinois to take my physical. The snow was piling up all about." Immediately, Dorothy found what others must have been finding: no one to welcome her, fortunately, an officer just returning from his three day pass helped by taking her to the hospital. And right away into the hands of a welcoming nurse, who helped get her to the Chief Nurses Office. Next, to, my, quarters. And afterwards in quick order she found as others, the change was to trucks. The following March she and the other nurses were bound for California.

She didn't know it then, but would be assigned to Camp Mc Coy in California.

One week later, she was in Long Beach, California. There, eighty-five other women found they were stationed as all of the G. I.'s (Government Issue) coming from throughout the United States. (In her case, that uniform was navy with a straight skirt and a white dickey fitted and even altered).

A significant event for her was receiving her uniform on a Friday in 1943. Furthermore, April 13th of that year she passed all of the entrance examinations. And that was when she became a 2nd Lieutenant as an RN... the reason the uniform I mentioned was so important to her, then she uttered, "I didn't have one because I was too short." It was a good thing for Sunday and, we fell, out, for inspection, but I didn't know what an inspection was, because I hadn't received any prior training, so I had to try and follow the leader." Those gallant girls certainly didn't know it then, but they were about to board the ship which on Monday they found was more, "Like a cattle car" was the way she described it. But a spirited group we were."

As to the voyage, it was sailing with no convoy, zigzagged across the Pacific Ocean the date that stood out was April 13th, the day we passed the International-Date-Line. Of course they didn't know they were bound for New Zealand, and Australia, where they would stop for one week. The deployment was, "God only knows where." Imagine it, they were at sea for a total of forty-two days. The gals were above on the top deck where the soldiers were beneath deck. "Fortunately, the conditions that the boys had to endure weren't anything as ours. We heard them as they told us of the bunks stacked one on top of another, extremely cramped, those suffering of sea sickness – the ones below had to deal with the fallout and the stench."

The next port was to be Bombay, India. It was that segment of the journey that seemed non-stop on the SS Hermtarp, I believed she called it, that hauled cargo "giving full steam…even though we thought we were going to fall apart for sure." And they knew they were being chased by submarines, and experienced a terrible storm at sea, with "talk about high seas." She added, "Even so, we arrived in Bombay, India and upon arrival we suffered the intense heat of 125 degrees. What she added was, "The girls were fainting due to the heat, fortunately the heat, didn't bother me, and there were many that got severely sea sick…I didn't."

I thought it was something the way she had such recall about the uniforms now to tell me of the summer uniforms they had. The stay for them there in Bombay was for one week.

"Ahead, we would be boarding three different ships which were by the British that led us to the Suez Canal." It wasn't hard to hear, "By now we thought we were on a trip to nowhere. All the time we were girls that were totally away from our homes for the first time caught in this mystical journey." Of all things she added, "We ran completely out of butter for our pancakes."

I thought when hearing this it is amazing after all of those years ago, this was still in her head on the tip of her tongue.

Next was the port of call boarding a train that, "had benches to set on…the, lavatory on the floor…which certainly didn't make it very easy for any of us, especially, with the train rocking back and forth," she added. This segment of the overall journey was to become a central point where the hospital had to be built, which was done in a hurry." On she went by saying, "We had tents to stay and sleep in…think of it, eighty-five women battling for time in the bath tubs, toweling down their bodies just to stay (somewhat) clean or have a cooler."

So, I would have a clearer picture I heard, "An appendectomy would be on a used table for the operation for the soldiers, sutures and all."

There were to be furthering destinations such as: Tehran at a depot. And if that wasn't enough, the hospital was built –had to be done hurriedly to shelter and enable them to work, care, nurse the boys in the five to six operating rooms. It was there we also took care of the natives in the region. "What was appalling was the lack of sanitation, with broken bones and lost limbs." All the time the heat was with us, HOT – HOT – HOT! Through all of it, was to come the desert conditions, "Down from away." Was the way she expressed it. Not just heat, also exhaustion, malaria and more and more heat. Conditions that were always with them were these among both the nurses and patients. Another that had to be dealt with was the 10 per cent disability. But the conditions included: spending two years in 120 degrees heat, dust storms, sand flies, scorpions and constant monotony. But there was more that she left out describing the scene. She, had described, how vital they were, to the war effort, and knew they would be remembered, for all, that they did. Further reading has brought me to find, some of the details that have to be included –

THE WAR
AN INTIMATE HISTORY
1941 – 1945
By – Geoffrey C. Ward and Ken Burns

They were scared to death. Really frightened
Half, out, of their, minds. I hugged them. I was
Teary eyed. It makes me cry to think of it…some
Of them were so unnerved that I just had to put
Arms around them and hold them…some, were,
Twenty-two and twenty-three even eighteen. It was
Terrible, it had to be done.

And all of the 'gallant girls,' were so vital to the war. This was
The region where men drove trucks from the Gulf to the Russian
Border, always, battling primitive conditions.

A personal experience came for Dorothy because near them was
a camp for displaced Polish women, children and old men. "Even
though none of us knew much Polish, I became friends with those
washing and cleaning for us. And the way we were able to help, was to
give them a Christmas party of candy bars, cigarettes and other gifts we
received from our homes in the states."

One very important vigil was remaining aware of the nomads from
the camel caravans, for if not watched, they would enter the hospital
wings and steal beds, sheets and pillows.

Another pronounced experience was December 1943, in Tehran
for a one week R & R. And she wanted me to know, "I happened to
be there the very day the young Shah Reza Pahlevi celebrated his 21st
birthday." It was followed by, more rest in Palestine. From then, we
shortly afterwards received additional orders to report to Lyons, France
a field hospital, where we remained until the end of the war in Europe.
Finally, in 1945, during the month of September, I was bound for the
United States on another Liberty ship to Newport News, Virginia.

Much of her story came as the sand storms she and the girls, as she
called them, experienced while there in the desert.

She told me of their being transferred "Out of bounds" to get a
permanent as today we were having to "Wrap our hair in foil" and
they ran out of foil, which brought them to more than the wrap, the
permanent after the shampoo and back to bangs. It was though, "Soup
to our hair waiting for the water."

Thinking back, when all of this began, Dorothy was so young and
was now working her station which was the 26th Field Hospital in this,
"No man's Land."

But the journey led to the final assignment which was in far away
Iran. And to hear that at the very end of the war, she and the other
girls/women of that time in the war, were nursing and caring for

Russian soldiers. I know your recall of it was a saga. What was the hardest then was the translation and having to use sign language to give the care needed. Through all of it, she was at the GNL assigned as an American nurse.

Fortunately, for Dorothy, she was relieved and returned to Florida. Where the other nurses she had been doing duty with were sent on to France.

Finally, came what had to be the final segment of her sojourn, that, took, her home to Rush City, Minnesota. And all she wanted to be was assigned to any hospital, but arranged and set up a pre-nursery care facility. Even there, she remembered during the coldest times of the year having to use light bulbs to keep babies warm beneath wooden boxes. And she couldn't imagine it, night shifts only eleven to seven a.m. in 1971.

From there her final move was to Kirkland to nurse there too. What startled me while talking with her was to hear at last – "Memory is wonderful. " Before I concluded, my doing more than interviewing, I heard her say, "Few people knew we were in Iran when the Shah was in power. Our country did what we could to liberate Russia from communism. The U. S. A. had done so much for many countries and received little or no help in return." Granted, this was one, nurses thoughts that I was hearing – reviewing from a card I received dated, April 28, 2003.

NOTES FROM TRIP TO CHINA

What is beautiful is not always good,
But what is good is always, beautiful.

This tale tied with Renda's (a good friend from many years) chronicle. It was about all she learned traveling to China. Every time I have the privilege to hear heartfelt stories, something is always on the faces of each sharing the details.

All of this began when she was attending Pacific Lutheran University in Tacoma, Washington. It was there she began her work studying the Chinese language, which she minored in as she gained her degree. It enabled her to travel in China for a six month trip, taking her to the large city of Chengdu – where the American University was. This was the sister school of PLU. She continued, "It was freezing, below the dew point when I arrived." I could have sworn she had returned, as I watched her appear to be saying, "burr", adjusting her sweater, for momentary warmth around her shoulder. I knew from the gesture, it really had to be cold while she was there. She said the sights stuck with her. They were vivid ones. She remembered the rats were as big as rabbits. To keep them out, she bought some duck tape for twenty-five dollars, and taped up every crack, to keep the vermin from entering her quarters.

While there she was able to travel and learned a great deal of the history of China.

The festivals were fascinating for her which helped her better know cultures and customs.

"The population was really something," she added. She had prepared by making sure to have $200.00 worth of toilet paper a real commodity needed. She had been warned of that before.

"Coal was the way they got their heat, and the dust was unbelievable," saying this she literally coughed. I could see how memorable her time had been. She was appalled how the spitting was practiced by all. "I found myself staring at them, disbelieving this behavior" with a, "ugh", at stating this. She went on, "I think I recall, the windows being round, so the evil spirits couldn't get through."

Renda went on telling me, "To keep my bike, everyone had to have locks. Yes, a bike lock was a very important safe-guard. For the demons, were going to get them, if not secured."

She continued, "And shortly afterward, to be exact, it was twelve weeks later when the government knocked our house down."

She paused, then exclaimed, "Rats and bicycling to school was hell. They had to have their bicycles with an equivalent of a license plate and registration." To top it, she had to carry her bike up and down five flights every day. Talk about different from home in the United States. Her room was a one person room.

The way she put it was, "Maids, were the young girls from the country-side that did the work, in order to make the money. Some of them could speak some English, but I communicated with them, which required mastery of sign language, or trying to give meaningful gestures."

She said, "A minimal number were able to attend college." Her travels revealed the primitive, dire conditions, such as how the water was contaminated with sewage from the soil.

A pointed reminder from her was, "We have a lot to learn, to remember all of the privileges we have, and to appreciate all we have in comparison."

"Yes, Chinese boys are daunted over there, opposed to how the women are treated so poorly in comparison. And the garbage on the ground brought hundreds about constantly sweeping up the street." What an impression I was gaining listening to her. "The coal dust was everywhere, even on the dirt floors – poor conditions, to say the least."

Through all of the sights and memories, times, glimpses while there, she came to love the people and remained in contact with them. Renda yearned to return, which she has done several times.

This was another moment for me, to gain a deeper awareness of another world-wide traveler.

SEARCH FOR HOMETOWN

*Happiness, resides not in passions and not
in gold; the feeling of happiness,
dwells in the soul.*
Democritus

When Susan, a fellow classmate of mine told me her life's story, it left me wondering how a young girl could have held such thoughts. I thought military families were more settled, though I was aware of the continual moving they had to do, port to port. Such variables as changes of home, friends, being settled for a time in her case, all of the amenities a part of her life would have left me thinking, she would be deeply content.

She said, "I grew up in the Navy." Others that I knew referred to themselves as "military brats." Not in Susan's case.

She shared, "I once read that military children, usually, give their hometown as the place they liked best, at least the place they lived last or longest." That was a fallacy in her case. Where, she lived in Seattle, Washington, at Pier 91, the Navy base, and what caught my attention, was it was the Admiral's Quarters.

To grasp all conveyed in her words, "When you move to a new location, the motto is, it's hard at first, but you'll get used to it, you'll make friends and come to like it." That also was anything but true for Susan.

I didn't get used to it," was the way she put it, more like a declaration. She was able to gain friends that became long lasting ones.

Her father was the Admiral, and hailed from the big state of Texas. She added, "My mother was also from Texas, a former teacher." Susan had a half brother and sister, but "I, was my parents' only child." She was eleven years old when she came to Seattle, and had been many other places, through the years prior. She had experiences living in: Washington, D.C., Kamakura, Japan, Bremerton, Washington, Guantanamo Bay, Cuba; even the Panama Canal Zone. Talk about well traveled, far more than most kids, that, was a certainty.

She told me she loved Cuba and Panama. There, she thrived on the warm sunny climate. "Of course we kids always ran barefoot, spent a lot of time riding our bikes, like all kids, climbed trees, and spent time at the pool and the beach." There, she was fortunate to be living in a real neighborhood with other kids attending a neighborhood school together.

Immediately, I realized there was a similar chord. It was deep inside her soul, a longing for much more. The move to Seattle brought on something that she wasn't expecting. She had moved away from friends she had for years. She had become a very lonely girl, and found it a bewildering time.

"Here, we returned to the United States from Panama, and our travels took us through New York City, to my loving aunt, Nettie Sue, who lived in Bloomington, Indiana. It was the Christmas time of the year." I knew, she felt as any kid would, the excitement and feeling how beautiful the trip was as they made way down the tracks, taking the train through all of the little towns that were already decorated for the coming Christmas. What a sight it must have been. This became her impression of the Midwest. It would turn out to be more of the search for that very home-town, she had wanted all of her life.

Isn't it something, how all kids, one way or another, seem to have much the same thoughts or dreams?

I wanted to tell you more of where she found herself at the Navy base, below Magnolia Bluff in Seattle. Her families' home was a beautiful colonial with gardens to enjoy and an expansive view. If you can imagine, seven bedrooms and bathrooms! And it was for the three of them. Not only was she lost, the home must have left all of them lost, just trying to find each other one room to the next.

"There were no neighborhood kids," she said. "I attended Magnolia Grade School, and continued on to Catherine Blaine Junior High School. Afterwards, I began my high school days at Queen Anne High across from the base."

Then, she began to share what life was really like, saying, "My life was very different from the children at school. Where they all rode the bus to school everyday, I had my own chauffeur. He was my father's, Marine driver that took me to school everyday." This brought me to think of the movie, "Sabrina" where Audrey Hepburn was the daughter of the chauffeur, and grew up knowing how different her life was.

"We had servants who did the cooking, cleaning, serving the food, even doing the laundry." Such treatment made her feel downright uncomfortable, because, it didn't feel normal, "It was because our family was never alone." They were always in the midst of the staff with visitors from the base at all times. No privacy at all, although Sundays were different, with no others present that day.

Her mother was with her friends. Susan was busy being a member of Girl Scouts, Campfire Girls, even the Church of the Ascension Youth Group. There still was the lack of the other kids in the neighborhood. "I did have two best friends, Kathie and Claire, but it still wasn't anything like Panama," was the way she wanted me to understand how it really was. She had years taking piano lessons, was accomplished, but "I didn't like playing for recitals." She was an excellent student, always aware of what teachers wanted, and had gained the knowledge of how to study and how to pass tests.

A big shift occurred. Her father retired. That brought on more unrest, having to move away from the base for the first time, no more servants or privileges as before.

Rather than have to move, her parents decided to stay in Seattle. They wanted her to complete Queen Anne High. There, she found much the same pattern, of friends coming and going, including her boy friend Bud. He happened to be the son of an Army Colonel who transferred to in San Francisco. Another big shift! I knew all about those changes occurring, while doing as she was, trying to stay in the same school. Even though Susan was a fellow classmate of mine, one year behind me, I knew other kids went through the same upheaval, at that important time in their lives.

If it wasn't enough, that Bud moved, so did two other close girl friends that were also military kids. Always the coming and going. Nothing was sustained, accept attending school. What she wanted most, and had the opportunity to do, was visit Bud and his parents. At home she always seemed 'left out of the decisions,' as when her parents decided to remain in Seattle, and bought a home right there on Magnolia. Once again, the similar pattern, the constant changing weather, always a big part of Seattle.

When she returned from San Francisco, and her visit with Bud and family, her mother had done what any girl of that age would not want: she had decorated my room in that small house in pink." I certainly understood how she felt, never asked or consulted, left out, everything, just happening. And PINK-I know you know, that, was not the color she would have preferred; however, finally Susan was in a neighborhood, a place she could fit.

While in high school, she had the same busy schedule, and was involved as many of the other girls with Mariner Scouts, Girl's Club and Traffic-Court. With it came depression. She knew she had to seek help to deal with it; and found she had more than depression she also had Seasonal Affective Disorder. This is very true of many in the Seattle area, what with the weather I mentioned, especially, all of the rain that seems to never stop in the winter months and beyond. Susan was a sunshine girl, and had been the entire time in Panama, and at the other naval bases they had been assigned to.

She and Lynn Sherman Rice her finest friend, made the decision, to attend the University of Arizona together. Her parents were against it. Then she said, "I made up my mind, to be in charge, of where I lived from then on. Ahead were Tucson, the University of Arizona, and plenty of sunshine."

There came real change. It included pledging for Alpha Phi sorority, to live in the sorority house, for a total of three years. Her major was psychology and biology. Susan graduated in 1964. She met her "sunshine boy," Max Gaither, Jr., who was a business major and a baseball pitcher. They were married in Tucson.

The crux of her story was the search for her hometown. She and Max moved to Topeka, Kansas, Max's home town. While visiting him she thought it was a perfect hometown. She liked Topeka, because it wasn't too large and had tree-lined streets, a friendly neighborhood, and above all, sprawling front porches throughout town. It was there, she, completed her teacher's certification in education, continued working at the Menninger Foundation as a senior research assistant. And to top it, she told me, "I really liked my position as well as the Foundation work." Finally settled, at, last!

This was during the Vietnam War; Max was drafted and later became a jet pilot. During the ensuing five years, their children were born. More travel was ahead, and to think she had finally found something she wanted most, "Her hometown" after all of those years. Next was Beeville, Texas, where Diana, was born. Their son, Rob was born, while on the Roosevelt Roads, Naval base in Puerto Rica. And believe it, or not, a return to the Navy way of life. Although, I thought of all of the travel she was experiencing.

This was only the beginning though. There didn't seem to be enough – for Pensacola, Florida, San Diego, California, Norfolk, Virginia; and bases that were anything but her favorite locations of: Meridian, Mississippi and Beeville, Texas; not to mention Puerto Rico. All atypical of what a Navy family would experience, yet away from all she had come to thoroughly want, to settle in her home town.

Susan, made up her mind she was returning to Topeka, Kansas, knowing that was the HOMETOWN for her, and besides, she was offered another position working for the Menninger Foundation, which more than thrilled her.

The kids were growing up and were good students and quite athletic. Diana was a basketball player, where Rob played football and baseball as his dad. They all had found their church. Susan attended, Kansas-State-University. It was to earn her, master's degree in Special Education, working with emotionally disordered students, teaching in the Topeka Public Schools. As a typical hometown girl, she became a member of Junior League.

In the meantime, her daughter graduated from Topeka West High School, and continued on to Kansas University. Once again, 'real life' happened with the passing of her parents. Susan found the passing of her mother very difficult, at the same-time she was diagnosed with degenerative-disc-disease. Needless to say, this impacted her life. It kept her from cooking, cleaning, exercising, dancing, and to stand was hard as well. Even traveling by train, buses and cars became difficult- nearly impossible.

Two years passed, and her son Rob graduated and of all things he decided to attend as Susan had, the University of Arizona. What came then as is true for many of us, the empty nest. Max, her husband, had an arthritic hip and then had to have hip replacement. He had always been a whiz, quite successful in handball and was no longer able to compete. She said, "Then came his losing money in risky business ventures, one after another, and finally, losing everything. He isn't that different than a myriad of others, and this writer submits, that I have nothing but high hopes for Max to find his way again professionally, to regain "the key to the office."

Depression and loneliness returned, all the time, Susan was pretending all was alright. The kids were graduating and doing wonderfully. They have gone on and become very self-sufficient.

Susan added, "I retired from teaching, because I was burned out after I was fifty-five years old." And as she continued, I thought the pattern wasn't unlike vast numbers of us. LIFE!

It became her destiny: to get involved in activities such as water exercise, some travel, being with her bridge partners, bible study, even a volunteer in her church and came divorce. Thinking back to the overall picture, of what her life had been like, I was anything but surprised, to hear how it turned out.

Today, she has remained in what came after all of the traveling that comes for many of us in our lives, to end her "SEARCH FOR HOMETOWN". She found it, in Topeka, Kansas. And to top it, she is a tutor and a pare-educator or teacher's aide and loves every moment of it.

So, from all Susan suffered as a girl – depression and more – to finally be able to light, and settle. She added, "I enjoy writing and periodically receiving phone calls." This writer is very glad for her, for "hometown" means a great deal for many of us as well.

And would you believe it the fog horns are blowing, all is enshrouded in the morning fog, and I know this writer is where he belongs, in what has become for him hometown also, in Tacoma, Washington. Say, I have a question for you. When considering your own life has it been so different?

PICK QUICK
A PLACE WORTH TRAVELING TO

While I was waiting for an order of one great double burger and a milkshake, I couldn't help but wonder why the MIA flag was displayed below our Red White and Blue National Flag.

A couple of the other hungry souls speculated as to the reason. In the meantime, I heard "Orders Up. "The man stepped up, paid, and thanked the ladies. It hit me that this spot would be perfect to write about.

There isn't a day the customers aren't congregating for their lunches. It is located in Fife, Washington.

I made an appointment to see the owner, Joe Burgi. He said, "My business has been blessed, after twenty-two years, for years ago there in Fife, there were forty-five drive-ins." He added, "Ours is the only one that remains."

I asked him why he thought they proved to have staying power, he said, "It's due to never changing the menu one bit. All was to ensure the food was the freshest and the service took top billing."

They knew from the start how important it was to keep the grounds clean. The spot has been an oasis. It was a respite for truckers and business people in the area. Would you believe there are regulars who come from, Montana? "The travelers from other bordering states and towns purposefully, stop too. It gives them a place to sit and talk for hours to catch up," was what Joe said. When they arrive they take a picnic table, clean, freshly painted, beneath an umbrella of a maple tree. Next to the parking area toward the front is a flowing dwarf flowering-cherry tree, which seemed to be perfect for the birds. Joe added, "I have been given offers from nearby nurseries of $1,500.00 for that tree if I decide to sell this prime location that my wife Betty and I established over the years." In the backdrop are fifty year old poplar trees reaching high to the sky.

He told me, "There in the foreground were fields where my wife used to pick beans." The MIA flag was given to him by the Harley and Gold Wing bikers. It was a reminder of those lost.

Over the years he has provided employment for college age students. He set up a program so there could be assured jobs each year, for the students returning from their colleges and universities and the local area.

When looking, you'll never see one of those young women without a smile. Joe's caring spirit for every employee's total safety, especially, when working evenings, is very evident. He added, "You'll want to return."

No matter what your direction you can't miss this special spot. There are bright red geraniums and yellow marigolds giving the entire place a lift. If you sit awhile, you'll see Joe watering the flowers, keeping the edging up to par, a staff-member out picking up papers, cleaning tables and benches, for others to stop and enjoy their choice of quality food and return to work.

One more thing is how he always tapes the front of the Sports section on the front window so all can read it while waiting.

"The hours have always been 1 a.m. to 8 p. m. open from March to October. He told me, "The whole place just gets too cold after November – February."

He continued, "I was really concerned over our being closed each year. One year, we opened on March 30th, and found our customers were ten deep, that was the last of that concern."

I wanted to add this story, it, was one of my first that I wrote for the *Federal Wa- News…and I intend on including more stories of Stainless Steel Diners - in each of the books to come.*

BETTY GRABLE and ALICE FAYE MADE ME DO IT

Joseph J. Zelazy, Jr.'s story began on September 10th, 1921, when he was born in Wilmington, Delaware.

Joe's dad worked in a leather factory as a glazer, where his mother kept busy caring for Joe Jr., along with three children as a housewife.

Year's later, Joe Jr., attended Wilmington High School, where he was a member of the football, basketball, and baseball teams.

Joe wanted me to know, "I left school early to help out by supporting my family."

He told me, "I graduated and began working as a brakeman on the Pennsylvania Railroad. The news broadcast came of "A Day in Infamy', bringing all of us to know Pearl Harbor, Hawaii was deliberately attacked by the Japanese."

"One Saturday afternoon after a hard week of work, I went to see my favorite movie stars, Betty Grable and Alice Faye, in a new motion picture; I sat there held in a magnetic state. I began to ask myself gazing at those gorgeous gals on the screen, what I was going to do with my life. And the question brought me to more than think, in fact, "I didn't enlist immediately after going to that movie. It was a couple of months later that I enlisted.

Perhaps a portion of my answer came from both of those starlet's. He said, "I guess you could say, Betty Grable and Alice Faye helped me do it. Anyway, I never forgot it. The day was July 2nd, 1942.

He told me he wanted to be a tail gunner in the Army Air Force. Instead, "I was first sent to Ft. Belvoir Virginia where I was to gain Combat Engineering and Basic Training.

I never intended to be an Engineer at all. I thought – I'm a smart guy, why should I just make $21.00 a month as a Buck Private in the U. S. Army." And what came of it was to try for Officer's Training School, which he did and passed the course requirements while at Ft. Belvoir, Virginia. Joe informed me, "The next eleven months were very educational and challenging to say the least. Upon completing the course, I graduated as a 2nd Lieutenant on January 20th 1943."

Time and events passed far quicker then, for our countries military service not only was building a strong Army, it was doing the same for all branches of the military. There was a big job ahead. All of the men and women knew it when they signed up and took the oath.

He said, "My first assignment was to the 63rd Engineer Battalion – 44th Division to be stationed at Ft. Lewis, Washington and that was January 1943." Joe continued by saying, "The next eleven months was a very educational and challenging to say the least."

And if there weren't enough changes in his life already, "I met Lorrayne, who became the love of my life in September 1943." The truth was that they as vast numbers of G.I.'s did the same and he added, "It was December 15th 1943 when I was transferred to Pittsburgh, California. We were there for future shipment to Europe as a replacement."

All of this came like a flurry. He paused and added, "Christmas of 1943 was when I called Lorrayne to come and join me so we could be married. We were married on January 8th 1944 in Pittsburgh, California. The turnabout was on the 15th of January, when I received my orders and departed for Europe (after one week of marriage)."

And imagine today while sitting with Joe he said, "We have just celebrated over sixty-three years of being married," to see joy and a prideful look on his face, while he told me, "It was wonderful, having all members of the family together at the same time."

As he continued saying, "It was soon afterwards I received my orders to leave for Chilsledon, England the 22nd day of December 1943. I was assigned to the 5th Engineers Combat Battalion – 1278th Engineers for extensive training. That training was so we could learn to build obstacles, bridges and varied structures that would enable our soldiers to penetrate the enemy."

He continued with, "We first completed all of the training and left for the shores of Weymouth, England to embark across the English Channel bound for our landing at Normandy, France on December 19th, thirteen days later than D-Day, June 6th 1944. The work included, "Construction – maintenance of facilities for movement and shelter of supplies for the troops. All that was ahead of us was constructing not only obstacles for the invasion forces similar to the ones that they would encounter on the assault beaches, various forms of bridges, how to remove mine-fields, conducted Engineers reconnaissance, operated quarries, gravel pits, pre-mix plants, gave assistance to hospitals, depots, dumps, cleared streets in cities, posted highway signs, and logging sawmill operations. Undoubtedly, you have heard other G.I.'s say as Joe did, "The war itself is nothing as you see in the movies." Until the Battle of the Bulge started on the 16th of December 1944 we were never in combat with the Germans. However, on that day we were assigned to the 28th Division Area, for direct support." He added, "Our unit was inserted for battle duty that was, more scary, than you can ever imagine."

Then he added, "Being on the front lines of contact for two days all hell broke loose. Lt. Christy injured his back and I was taking Christy back to C.P. and was bringing the Mess Detachment and Communications with me. While returning to our forward battle stations, we were surrounded by German Paratroopers that stopped us blocking the road with a tank from the 747th U. S. Army Artillery unit, with 50 caliber machine guns. There was no where else to go. We had it!"

"My jeep driver, our radio operator and I were lined up against the wall and all of us were shot. In my case my left shoulder and we were left

155

for dead." In fact he said, "about 11:00 a.m. Germans officers arrived, turned us over and had us led into a building and beat and slammed us about, and I was thrown into a 6'8' deplorable room, which to this day I have never forgotten." He abruptly submitted, "The purpose was to hold me in solitary, constantly taking me out for interrogation." Then he paused and caught his breath and said, "Thinking back and tank that was blocking the road didn't take any more prisoners, instead they shot and murdered every one of the. That's warfare!"

His account continued, "Later on that day, thirteen of us were put in trucks, hauled to a train station that took us to Lemburg, Germany to Oflagg "XIIA." More needed to be said, "Once again I was thrown into solitary for ten days continually being interrogated twice every day. I didn't receive any medical treatment; instead, they continued the torture and left me wondering what was ahead."

Then he added, "We were taken aboard a train that continued on to Schubin Spelt, Poland and fortunately, we survived many air raids while there."

"We arrived in Koblenz, Germany the early part of January 1945, where Oflag 64 had about 1500 American prisoners. This was where the ball bearing factory was located." He added, "We were held hundreds of feet below the ground, all the time the bombs were colliding and hitting the factory."

In Joe's case he wanted me to know, "I wasn't forced to work and the reason was, I claimed I was a student and never employed for a trade." The treatment received by the prisoners included, "Soup and dark bread once a day, absolutely, no Red Cross whatsoever."

What was noticeable to me was how he had such recall regarding all that happened years ago. He went on and said, "At the end of January 1945, the Russians offered their offense to the war. It was then that the Germans arrived at the decision that we should start evacuating camp marching towards Berlin."

Wait until you hear as to this march. "It included: walking for two-hundred-and thirty-miles, in a total of twenty-eight days, in monstrous weather. There is no way I can explain how we dealt with these intense hard-ships."

I want to emphasize the solid stand they took. "After crossing over the estuary there were a couple of us who arrived at the decision, "We had enough." He told me that he made sure they knew, "I've walked enough and don't intend to do anymore, knowing that decision could be our doom."

When hearing I thought, hadn't they gone through enough?

No – "They put us on a train that was to take us to Luckenwalde, Germany. This was Stalag III, A, south of Berlin. That stay turned out to be peaceful, even quiet. The worst was – "We had no food!"

Fortune was with them without question.

"Russia liberated us in April and what a relief this was," was the way he shared it.

His account conveyed how much one of our guys had to face. Lastly, Joe submitted, "Russia wanted to take us through Odessa, Russia, Lt. Stevens and three Norwegian officers and I decided very early we were going to leave the camp. Then, we walked forty-four miles in three days to the American lines – TO FREEDOM!"

The great fortune was we met the 104th Division, were flown afterwards to, "Camp Lucky Strike" at La Havre for processing to return home to the good old U. S. A.

Now you and I would have thought all of this enough, but when arriving in New York City, New York he called home. At the other end of the line was his mother-in-law, Clara who absolutely didn't believe it was him on the other end of the line. But he finally brought her to believe it was him.

It would have been more than understood that Joe could kick up, have some long needed R & R upon return, but he had a lot to do, to care for his wife and soon his family. He emphasized with me he didn't get out of the service though.

In Joe's case he later began his own General Contractor business – drawing from his past experience, developing all to the success for the years to come.

His story doesn't end with this, it has continued with the VET that has and is in the process of: having gotten approval designing, what has already unfolded a grand effort of having built walls depicting which reveals, "The American Ex-Prisoners of War." And he continued telling me, "I'd like to see that the Coachella Valley American Ex-Prisoners of War would be recognized by plaques depicting them that served gallantly, as they did through WWII or any war."

And today Joe has organized POW Chapter, July 2002 – thirty-two members, actively involved in one form or another where they will be able to review to the public, "Our Wall – November 2007. " There is considerably more to be said of this after explaining other tasks they are doing.

Their efforts have included making sure VETS and their families are paid the respect as The Padres have proceeded to issue passes to all local and Southern California POW'S from the Korean (Police action) and War World War II, VETS may be honored and much more. A point of emphasis was hearing, "We started a database of about six-hundred names, even though many were deceased."

Today in the Pacific Northwest the Rainier's, and Emerald Downs Race track and the Saber cats honor the VETS as well as the Sonics, and the Seahawks. They're making sure the EX-POW'S and their families have free tickets to see the games.

Most recently, all that Joe has done is above and beyond by all of the work he has done and continues doing. Credit must be given to Meghan Erkkinen, of the Tacoma Weekly for her coverage explaining all in detail of his ambitious undertaking. Erkkinen wrote, "Many others will be honored for their service, sacrifice in a new memorial commemorating POW'S MIA'S at the Tacoma's War-Memorial-Park."

Joe went on and shared how he was proud was others that this was being completed this very week thanks to: Washington state Veterans of Foreign Wars (VFS) the Christmas Town chapter, of American Ex-POW'S.

This is his way of making sure all remember all their service for our country. Joe believes these have been totally neglected through the years. What he said next certainly caught my attention. For he said, "Once they're gone, they're gone."

More needed to be brought to the publics attention. They faced challenges in getting needed assistance for the project. Granted, twenty families of former POW'S and MIA'S contributed and hoped for tiles for the memorial wall the year past, even so, Joe did not get the support needed to complete the project bringing him to return all of the money and start all over "from scratch,"

By returning to the Washington state VFW and the Christmas Town chapter of ex-POW'S he found the support he needed to continue the project. The project was to sell personalized engraved ceramic tiles to place on the memorial wall. And the response has been favorable.

He has been pleasantly pleased at the response well beyond the 40 – 45 which he originally thought would be a fine beginning. He added with relish, "Receiving them from all over "it's unbelievable – a variety of their tours of duty." I was impressed hearing that the result already was 67 tiles. All of this effort was to be completed, September 19th and he is open to receiving orders so to add more tiles as the interest grows. Atop the wall will be, "Wall of Honor" all in gold letters. In the center will be two-foot-three-foot designs of an eagle. And surrounding it will be "the purchased tiles". Each to read, their names of former POW'S or MIA'S of their service. The difference is that details are included not just their names. By doing this, will provide, historical context for the young to read and pay respect toward.

I know having gotten to know Joe, it's my hope all will further educate the kids of this vital time of our countries history.

As stated, September 19th of 2008 was to be the dedication of the wall.

What will be viewed will be: black granite 6" x 6" tiles on the wall, all with names of Pierce County, POW/MIA. To list name, rank, branch of service and other information.

This VET has been guided by "Impossible Is Not A Fact, It Is, an Opinion" which certainly describes him.

Today he is a Lt/Col who began as a 1st Lieutenant CE U. S. Army 1944 WWII. Battle of the Bulge POW 21 Dec. 44 – 25 May Stalags 12 A & 3A Oflag 64. It has been far more than a privilege to share his account with you.

Although there is one more vital thing that truly rounds out his story and I was fortunate to gain this as well. To best share it if I may, these are the words expressed by his loving wife, Lorrayne.

"Wife's Feelings When Missing"

She wrote the following: It has been a long time ago – but I know I never felt that the wouldn't come home – I prayed everyday, and had faith –and the Good Lord granted my prayer-Of course, we were worried – he was captured Dec 21st and I didn't hear then from him for about 3 weeks – (he was very good about writing & so I was more than concerned, especially reading the papers and following the war, then on January 8th which was our first wedding anniversary the telegram came. I was living with my folks and so my mother called at work to say I had a telegram from Joe. I asked her to open it and read it – there was a silence and then my mother said, "I will come down and give it to you" – then I knew something was funny. And, of course it informed me that Joe had been missing in-action since Dec. 21st – I never heard another word until Joe called me from New York – He was home in Tacoma when the telegram for the Red Cross came, saying, he was a POW. But as for feelings – life went on – I worked everyday – and many people, were going through the same thing. However, it was always on my mind. I know I lost 25 lbs. in 5 months, which was OK.

Family – friends – work and faith get you through.

I knew hearing this from her rounded out the story best for I felt hearing her thoughts truly told their total story.

Today, he and those like him are as he, eighty-five years old or more and counting, but comparatively strong, enthusiastic and able to share his story with one and all.

To have had this opportunity, when thinking of it is more as a gift, to just have him share his account in the deepest of detail with me, has been my honor. More than that, to be able to share it with all of you – hoping, his depiction will bring you to know far more of how he and those of "The Greatest Generation" survived all they had to go through.

WITHOUT A DOUBT A FUTURE OLYMPIAN

"Karina Schwartznau was born, March 7th, 1995; some might say she, has been deemed from the start to be all that I am sharing." Her hometown is, Bonney Lake, Washington. When I met her she was twelve years old. One more thing I want to point out, this was in her words.

After you read her account, you'll be able to see a future Olympian to enjoy kicking up crystalline sprays of snow, as she ably plies down the slope.

"Before I was born my parents were snow skiers. When I was born and nine days old; I was at the top of Crystal Mountain, Washington.

At eighteen months my parents put me on skis and that's when I started skiing, in no time I became better and faster. From there I skied about thirty days a year.

When I turned five years old I joined the Crystal Mountain Alpine Club (CMAC), a race team our mountain provides. I wanted to try it out. When I raced I won my first race. I decided that I wanted to continue ski racing. I started out on the Saturday program. It was during the half season, when my parents switched me, because I wanted to be more competitive."

"Both of my parents realized, their support, would be needed throughout. They were sure I had the talent, viewed I would not only improve, there was no doubt I would become more than one that competed, among the others in the club."

She continued, "The next year my grandpa passed away and it was very tough. He was buried in a place so every time we went up to Crystal Mountain, we said, "hello," as we passed his burial site."

"The year after that, I had my first major fall, but all my friends supported me, I still got ninth place out of about twenty girls."

"We race against our own sex and age. The year after my injury I won nearly every race. I started to train on Wednesdays of every week right after school. My dad drove me to train, at Snoqualmie Pass.

Last year, I started to train on Saturdays and Sundays, I also added Wednesday nights. Racing got very competitive. I won the Warm Up, Slalom and got second and fourth place in the Cherry Tree Charge. I was selected to be on the Buddy Werner Team, the best of the best in the Northwest, including the mountains in Washington, Idaho, and Oregon. There were about one-hundred twenty nine, girls, I was competing against in the slalom. I got eighth place.

In the summer time, I go to the gym, lift weights, play soccer, run track to stay in shape and to get stronger. I also attend summer camps at Mt. Hood in Oregon. My goal is to become an Olympic Gold Medalist ski racer.

She added, "I don't just have one hero, I have three. The first is, Libby Ludlow. I actually have met her. She is a hero because she followed her dreams and made it to the Olympics. She started where I began, skiing at Crystal Mountain at a young age. The second is a coach of mine, Alan Lauba. He was on the U.S. Ski Team, now a coach. He is friendly and helps us be the best racers we can be.

The third is my dad. He was a racer but now he just free skis. He helps me and supports to help me get in shape, buy all my equipment, waxes my skis for race day. He and my mom, Wendy, pay for my ski camps. He has always been there for me supporting me to my goals. He is like my personal pit crew. He takes me up to the mountain every weekend and training on Wednesday's after school. He is a fast skier, but also a loving, caring father. If I was to ever get hurt, either physically or mentally, I know he would be there for me."

I know Karina's mother is more than there for her daughter. She fully supports all that her daughter is striving to achieve each and every week.

Parents such as these are so needed, so that a child can reach her dream. I am more than certain we will see this young lady in the future Olympics. She'll be there for the youth of tomorrow as a guide, undoubtedly as a coach for others, similar as she has had.

Today she competed in the Giant Slalom and told me, "It's one of my 'best' events. Not only that event, also the Super Giant Slalom, to hear her exclaim, "I'm definitely aiming for the Olympics in the future." I asked her a key question. What did she like the most about the sport and all she has learned? To hear, "It's all because, I like to go fast!"

Even though I wasn't able to see her in person, I somehow could hear on the ski slopes, in the distance, "I know I can do it." This is one person who will do more than try to be there when her day comes to compete in her first Winter Olympics. Her dream is far more than that. She is going to earn the right to drape that Gold Medal, around her I am sure.

Karina makes sure to set the bar higher every time she enters and competes. It is no wonder she already has achieved a record time of 59.42 seconds, recording a fastest time for any girl or boy in what she called the J4 classification.

And the records aren't left on the slopes; she excels at the Lakeridge Middle School as an honor student.

Karina has a total absence of fear. Unlike the other kids, she keeps cranking up to ski faster each and every day. Why? You might ask. Her reply is, "The faster I go the more fun I am having."

Watching her you know without question, especially considering what I shared already, she was born to ski. And you might appreciate, Karina's goals have caused, her to forgo lots of birthday parties, social events, and she never sleeps in on weekends. Believe me, she knows that to be all she aspires, she must pay the price, in order to totally be successful in the sport, keeping her grade point more than average, all, is as though "when I am not skiing, I'm studying."

Believe me when hearing her mentor, Alan Lauba say, "I look at her as a star pupil." She is a very solid skier, with her attitude, work ethic, following the right path, and if she later competes well at the NCAA level, she will do quite well."

I quickly realized she was the kind of a student that tended to absorb what she learns as a sponge, always absorbing every bit of it.

Other key ski events that she surely would compete and excel in are the J3 Olympics at Bogus Basin, Idaho, a Pacific Northwest Ski Association sponsored event. "If I win at the Buddy Werner, there is a better chance for my gaining a sponsor, which would help me have ski lift passes for a whole year." And believe me, I knew that would be important for her, for having a sponsor would help as she skied seventy-six times on the slopes this year, enabling her to keep getting better and better.

And to sum up her story consider what a recent article quoted about her in the Ski Club Spotlight magazine. "The club's current up-and-comer is J4 Karina Schwartznau, whose slalom technique is the best the staff has seen, at that age."

To prove all, I just heard, Karina was going to compete at the next J3 Junior Olympics at Brundage Mountain near McCall, Idaho. What a start for the future Olympian doing a whole lot more than plowing downhill wherever she is competing.

> And not only is it vital to thank Karina
> For her words as written, also to credit both
> From: Ski Club Spotlight
> "Building Technicians"
> By – Vanessa Pierce
> And
> The Enumclaw and Bonney Lake Courier – Herald
> Wednesday, February 27, 2008
> "Schwartznau's ski career picking up speed"
> By – John Leggett

Of – The Courier Herald

Thanks to their pieces.

This story could be for those of you following, The Junior-Olympics and the Winter-Olympics soon to come for all of us to enjoy.

A DIAMOND IN THE ROUGH

Perhaps one would say Classmates Reunion is a "Diamond in The Rough," but no matter what the description, when taking a poll, it's a gift discovered by thousands, even millions. This gift is a linkage to something many people did not realize was a gap in their lives or as something missing. And now the gap can be filled or someone found, merely by taking the simple steps that are part of what the founders designed.

They are here in the Seattle-Tacoma region. I found this out through a very good friend as she was the same with the founders. I told her I was having success finding of my friends from the past through this means.

My discovery was not only finding, but learning to use this, which I could only think of as a "Diamond in the Rough." And the search has continued locating friends from high school, college, jobs, fellow Airmen – veteran brothers of yesterday.

The truth is Classmates Reunion has been a way to discover something that has been deeply missed for all too long. This began for me nearly four years ago. Happily, I was able to reconnect with friends that were lost in the collage of the yearbooks. What has come from this search, have been feats by one and all. Immense growth!

Some of their progress has included: one making way with other sailors from Halifax, Nova Scotia to sail through the Northwest Passage all the way to Alaska another which entertains in senior homes through the country, the husband and wife that play Ragtime Piano for the same enthusiasts. Other findings were: to determine brother – friends still producing financial guides for their clients, one working with ecology and related services, two delving into the Realty – Land Development work, one who participated not only in athletics while attending college, but went even farther to the NFL to play Professional Football for his career – now retired, the date from my Senior Prom that has been living in Denmark for some forty plus years who lived on a farm raising Christmas trees, nurses that have served well in the health – sciences throughout the world, to hear of all points on the globe that many have frequented, those that have served in governmental positions, musicians that continued in the arts, others that have working galleries, another who found herself in the glass forms of artwork and sales, retired executives, one that coached and found his true love of working with training dogs and showing them through the years, talking with teachers from yesterday, those who became wonderful artists. You'll read of another who with her husband found the passion working with the rail road achievement program in the Las Vegas area, one more that switched direction, as many of us taking him into the mining engineering professional career field, one owning his own automotive parts business.

What has impressed me most, is, to realize that those of our class and I am sure of yours, have prospered professionally and personally since our days together back in the hallways and classes we attended. I even uncovered a friend that was anything as myself, called, "The Three Musketeers" who shared their quips and fun with all who knew them.

No matter, if they were of Marin County, California or the surrounding area it's become a wonderful experience for me and undoubtedly has been for you.

If you can imagine some fifty years later, finding all of the people is what can and does happen for others every day making the process intended more than important.

Two were found by sailing across the bay from San Francisco to the Larkspur Landing, to disembark; they were standing to meet my wife and me that hadn't been seen or talked with since 1959 – 1961. All of us gave each other a big hug and had our own reunion which lasted for some five hours. Lots to talk about and today, exchanging emails, cards, even gifts, is overwhelming.

We met on one occasion in Sacramento, California to tour the Old Train Museum, later to enjoy a longer period of time while lunching next to the Sacramento River, an opportunity to catch up with one another.

Sadly, to hear of too many no longer with us that can be counted.

I hope all of you are experiencing much of the same. For these encounters will, I promise you, make for a more rounded way of life today and tomorrow.

All of this has been like finding a "Diamond in the Rough."

FOR SOME GOLF AND FISHING IS ENOUGH

Others might say, no
It's two for-the Rails

Traveling throughout the country there remains the hollowing whistle pouring out, all it takes is to look down the track and there she blows. No matter where in the country railroad tracks are there for all of us to cross.

This is an account none of you would believe I assure you. Where retirees are out on the links, or fly fishing on their favorite streams, they have even left signs on their doors, or still noted to have "gone fishing or golfing" after their years on the earth, seldom, will you read a story as this one.

Throughout the country are Rail Road museums as the one I am about to tell you of, as the memorable display of the trains in Sacramento, California even in Enid, Oklahoma to name only a few.

What caught my attention regarding all of this was to think that one, a 66-year old former Boeing Company secretary and her husband 65 year old retired Boeing Engineer who designed flight safety systems, that kept an aircraft's engines running in case there was a failure, as retirees became involved today as evolving Engineers, in the history, of the Nevada State Railroad Museum's Southern Division. Now how's that, for an active couple, doing just that, remaining active and productive? They live in Henderson, Nevada as retirees, which began by Roger Himka coming for a three-day consulting job, now to live there in Henderson since 1993, to find they have stayed for fifteen years.

And when you hear their story and all that they have achieved, you'll know they'll probably remain there for the rest of their days. You'll find quickly how they have and continue to spend their weekends through the year. It isn't on the links or in any stream.

And when thinking how prior this couple were involved with car clubs, particularly British cars, with Bonnie Himka driving her Jaguar, they began to draw from their untied background with an interest in trains, since in Roger's case as a kid, and Bonnies fondest memories of trains as a child, watching them during the Christmas Holidays, and riding trains from Seattle to Portland, Oregon. Wait now to find where all of that took them.

To gain this story is more than that alone. Bonnie happens to be a fellow student and friend from years ago while attending the old Warren Avenue Grade School on Queen Anne Hill in Seattle, Washington, between the years of 1952 – 1954 on to Queen Anne High at the top of the hill for work while in high school. And now all those years later, to be sharing this account with all of you is my privilege.

Before jumping the track, let me explain how this came about not only for the two of them, more importantly, for those frequenting that available for them too.

As years in the past with the Union Pacific railroads "played an important part of…Nevada history." When thinking of this, in truth, miles and miles of track existed throughout Nevada. All of this has come about as a way to save and restore trains and rail that connected the communities there in the earlier years. One train, a spur of the track is the Boulder Branch Line which is now preserved and maintained by the Nevada State Railroad Museum in Boulder City, Nevada.

Some of what Bonnie and Roger had to learn was, "High ball to Railroad Pass" which came to know as, "All clear to leave the station towards the Railroad Pass." Just some of the terminology, that had to be learned through the years. Their interest has taken them being promoted and wearing varying hats: first as car attendants, rear brakeman, front brakeman, conductor, and now becoming Engineers in training. So from blue-and-white striped overalls, to all of the uniforms for each job while learning all entailed within each capacity.

What I have enjoyed most is seeing and hearing them talk of all about volunteering they have found in their community. For instance talking with Bonnie, she was overjoyed at the results of this day. She said, "We were able to gain over $2,000.00 from those riding the train and over $1,500.00 for the gift shop.

It's important to repeat in case I forgot to share with you they are the first married couple as an Engineer team in the Nevada State Railroad Museum's Southern Division. And to think their involvement started about eleven years ago.

That was due to their visit to see the Great American Train Show at Cashman Field, then on to what they told me, Opportunity Village, where ironically they ended up as an engineer for the Magical Forest Train." That alone took them down the track there for ten years.

So you could say they cross-trained. And when Bonnie became a conductor she became known as one with "wonderful rapport, courteous, delightful, with a great attitude." She has become an asset for all they are doing for the railroad and that isn't hard to believe. (What is really interesting is thinking of her in the younger years, one of the quiet ones in our class, downright shy)

When you think of all they have to learn and practice it is worthy for all they have achieved. She told me, "learning about locomotives and rolling stock is very different, for they have had to come to understand a trains brakes and how they work, how to start the generators for the air-conditioning system, know all of the safety procedures, how to start the train, even how to work the whistle because every whistle means different things to all working on the railroad.

Take the brake system alone. Bonnie shared, "working on getting comfortable with the braking system to provide an easy ride, that the locomotive in fact other cars have braking systems that must be in sync for a smooth stop. She added, "its, all a challenge."

What they both emphasized was extremely meaningful for me though. "All of it gives them a chance to play with the trains and do community service at the same time." After all, isn't that what all of us want most in our lives at that vintage and above?

Historically this in retrospect: "The train used to deliver materials and equipment from Las Vegas to Boulder City to the rim of the Black Canyon during the construction of Hoover Dam in the early 1930's. The last of the large generating units for the dam were installed in 1961. Shortly afterwards, the tracks were donated to the state," but today, a seven-mile roundtrip is what remains of that original route that was used by the Union Pacific Railroad and the U.S. Bureau of Reclamation.

Now it's a 45 minute trip, scenic with complete narration for the passengers, and it includes: refurbished Pullman cars, dated back to 1911, the rolling stock was acquired in 1993 from, "Heber Creeper" in Utah. Its capacity is for 250 passengers with two of the Pullman-cars, now with armchair seats, a roofed open-air car, even closed that is ADA accessible with a lift. Yes, even a dining car – memorably the best way to dine ever – and a kitchen.

To think that both the train and track receive "tender loving care" from the pool of fifty or more volunteer as Bonnie and Roger Himka, all so proud to be involved as they are through the year.

Just to give you an idea as to the service they are providing the passengers through each year includes of all people: Santa Claus and the riders count has gone from 871 who rode first at the opening in 2004 to 18,569 in 2007 and believe it, for 2008 the number has gown to 20,000, developing into begin open for all to ride on Saturdays and Sundays through the year.

All of this is for one and all to experience real nostalgic memories of all those days before. And by riding the train the experience includes what the Southern Nevada Railway Museum is, one of seven state funded museums to enable everyone to visit other state railroad museums in Carson City and Ely, Nevada.

To think, because, Bonnie and Roger chose to do more than golf or fish. Their doing so they hear many times, "This is my first time to ride a train" by the children, coming aboard. By doing this they get to look out of the panorama of the Eldorado Valley, the mountains, even down into the Railroad Pass Hotel and Casino. Talk about exciting the ride includes: starting at the rail yard near Yucca-Street, and continues on through five tunnels through the mountain rock which has been turned into a hiking trail for families to enjoy.

So, if you want to meet two Engineers on the railroad head for Las Vegas and surrounding area – there will be Engineer Bonnie and Roger Himka.